DEAD IS JUST A RUMOR

marlene perez

G RAPHIA

Houghton Mifflin Harcourt

Boston   New York   2010

www.hmhbooks.com

The text of this book is set in Adobe Jenson.

Library of Congress Cataloging-in-Publication Data
Perez, Marlene.
Dead is just a rumor/Marlene Perez.
p.   cm.
Summary: Psychic teen Daisy Giordano has her hands full trying to
find out who is behind the blackmail letters being sent to paranormal residents
of Nightshade, while also worrying about her werewolf boyfriend going away to
college and the possibly lethal cooking lessons she is taking with a sinister chef.
[1. Supernatural—Fiction.   2. Psychic ability—Fiction.   3. Werewolves—Fiction.
4. Sisters—Fiction.   5. High schools—Fiction.   6. Schools—Fiction.]   I. Title.
PZ7.P4258Ddj   2010
[Fic]—dc22   2009050010
ISBN 978-0-547-34592-5 (pbk. original: alk. paper)

Printed in the United States of America
DOM 10 9 8 7 6 5 4 3 2 1
4500241884

To Michael, for all the moral (and tech) support

CHAPTER ONE

"I heard a rumor about you," Penny Edwards said to me. The gym was crowded and noisy, so I had to move closer to hear what she had to say. The girls' volleyball team was practicing at one end and Samantha was at the other end, barking orders like a gorgeous blond drill sergeant. I couldn't hear Samantha from where I stood, but whatever she said sent her minions scurrying.

I smothered a sigh. Penny had never been one of my favorite people, but I thought she'd changed over the last few months. Apparently, I was wrong.

"What rumor?" I said, not really wanting to hear the answer.

"That you and Ryan are shoo-ins for king and queen of the Midnight Ball." She smiled at me and I caught a glimpse of the kinder, gentler Penny.

"I hope not," I said. "Samantha's been working really hard on the ball. I hope she and Sean win." Samantha Devereaux was my best friend, who for a time had been my worst enemy — or at least a thorn in my side — and was back to being my best friend again.

We'd been through a lot during our junior year at Nightshade High, but I was expecting smooth sailing for our senior year. Or as smooth as it could be, considering that we lived in a town that was a little different, to say the least.

"Samantha's definitely a contender," Penny said. "Especially since everyone who is a resident of Nightshade gets to vote."

"Well, please tell everyone I don't want another crown." Last year, I'd been crowned homecoming queen in a bizarre turn of events. I didn't want to sound ungrateful, but that was enough glory for me. Samantha thrived in the spotlight. I did not. Now that she and I were finally friends again, I wasn't going to let some tinsel crown come between us.

Penny gave me a half wave and headed to the locker room. I watched her go.

"Daisy, look out!" Samantha warned me as a giant orange jack-o'-lantern rolled down the aisle. I put out a hand and concentrated. It rolled to a stop in the nick of time and narrowly missed squashing me flat.

You had to stay on your toes when you lived in Nightshade, and having psychic powers helped. I looked around the gym to see if anyone had noticed my public psychic slip, but everyone's attention was on the volleyball game going on at the other end.

"Halloween is over a month away, you know," I said, gesturing toward the bright decoration.

Samantha peered at me from behind a huge box of orange and black streamers, cardboard black cats, and ghosts. "It's not just any Halloween," she replied. "It's Nightshade's two hundredth anniversary celebration. I'm one of the chairs."

"I know. I was just telling Penny how hard you've been working." Samantha volunteered for practically every committee the high school had. Now that it was finally our senior year, she didn't seem to be slowing down at all.

"Gotta go!" I said, as I remembered the other thing Sam liked to do, which was rope me into volunteering for whatever pet project she was involved in. I'd wait for Ryan somewhere far, far away from my volunteering-happy friend.

"Don't you dare take a step out that door, Giordano!" she said, only half teasing.

I repressed a sigh. Sam was unstoppable. Besides, I had to admit, I had fun when I was around her. At least, most of the time.

"I have plans for those psychic powers of yours," she continued. "How else are we going to hang these decorations on the ceiling?"

"Okay, if you promise not to try to squash me with a squash again."

"Who's trying to murder you this time?" Ryan said. He put his arm around me and gave me a hello kiss. My boyfriend was the best thing about senior year, although I had to push away the thought of what would happen to us once we graduated. I'd worry about that when the time came.

"Hi, Ryan," Sam said. "Where's Sean? He promised me he'd help." Sean was Samantha's boyfriend and Ryan's best friend.

"He's still in the locker room," Ryan replied. "But he mentioned you guys might need another hand."

Samantha's momentary irritation at her boyfriend disappeared. "Can you haul these outside?"

Ryan took the box from Samantha. "Where do you want these?"

"I rented a truck," she replied. "It's in the first stall in the parking lot." The first stall in the parking lot was Principal Amador's, but if anyone could get away with commandeering his spot, it would be Samantha.

Sean walked up, carrying a green gym bag under his arm.

"What took you so long?" Samantha said.

"Sorry, babe," he replied. "I got caught up talking to Wolfgang."

She made a face. "What were you doing talking to *him?*"

"He's helping Coach with the stats," Sean said. "I can't ignore him."

"Why not?" she replied. "After what he did this summer, he deserves to be ignored."

Wolfgang Paxton was a freshman who had been giving

some of the football players a little something extra in their Wheaties, and the summer had ended with half the football team becoming werewolves. The ones who weren't already, I mean. Fortunately, the side effects of Wolfgang's "hairballs" turned out to be temporary.

"Don't worry," Sean said, soothing her. "He's calmed down since the summer."

Samantha held out her hand. "Keys, please. I need to take this stuff to the Wilders."

Sean opened his bag and dug through the contents. He didn't notice when a heavily embossed envelope fell out and landed on the polished floor.

I stooped down and picked it up. I wasn't trying to be nosy, but the blood-red wax seal aroused my curiosity. It looked like a fancy invitation, with creamy white stationery that was silky to the touch.

I handed it to Sean. "That's not mine," he said. He shoved the envelope into a pocket, then peered into the bag. "I must have grabbed the wrong bag." He hurried off to the locker room.

He returned a few minutes later, carrying an almost identical gym bag. "I grabbed Wolfie's by mistake."

Sam checked her watch. "C'mon," she said. "We're late."

Ryan and I just stood there until Samantha barked out, "Are you coming?"

"Coming where?" I said.

"The Wilder mansion," she replied. "I'm storing stuff there until we can clean up the haunted house."

"What haunted house?"

"That old deserted mansion up by the Wilders — Merriweather House. It's going to be the centerpiece of the town celebration. We're having the Midnight Ball there. It's supposed to be haunted."

"It sounds . . . monumental," I said aloud, but I was thinking that it sounded like a monumental amount of hard work. Everyone in town knew the dance would be the culmination of the anniversary events, but I had just assumed it would be held at the Wilder estate, which was the biggest, fanciest place in town.

After loading the truck, Ryan and I got in his car and followed Samantha and Sean to the Wilder estate.

"How's your dad?" Ryan asked.

"He's . . . okay," I said.

"That bad, huh?" Another thing I loved about Ryan. He could tell what I really wanted to say, without me having to say it.

"He's getting better, but he's still . . ."

"Distant?" Ryan guessed.

I nodded. "He says he doesn't want to talk about it." My dad had been through a traumatic experience. Most of Nightshade had thought he'd run off with another woman, but the truth was he'd been abducted and held captive by the Scourge, an anti-paranormal group. Mom had rescued Dad from their clutches, but not until he had been gone for six long years.

Dad hadn't left the house much at all since his return. Mom had made a few tentative noises about him going back to teaching, but he hadn't even called his old department at the university. He even talked about writing a book, but I hadn't seen any evidence that he was actually working on it.

The Wilder mansion was one of the oldest places in Nightshade. We pulled up the long driveway and parked. There was a restaurant on the property, but it only took up a minuscule part of the main house.

Samantha rang the doorbell, and it was the elegant Mrs. Wilder herself, the elderly matriarch of the shifter clan and the owner of the estate, who answered the door. She pointedly looked at her watch and said, "We start serving dinner in one hour."

"We'll be finished by then," Samantha promised.

"Excellent," Mrs. Wilder replied. "Bianca will show you the way."

Bianca materialized from the shadows. Bianca worked at Wilder's Restaurant, but her duties didn't end there. Bianca was a shape-shifter, too. She took the form of a sweet-looking black kitten, but looks could be deceiving.

Instead of the severely chic dresses I was accustomed to seeing her in, she was dressed in jeans and a sweatshirt. She still managed to look gorgeous. A familiar-looking envelope with a red seal was shoved into the back pocket of her jeans. Interesting.

"Hi, Bianca," I said.

"Daisy," she said. "Did you get your letter already?"

"Letter?" I said, confused. My mind flashed to the heavy envelope Sean had dropped earlier.

"You haven't received it yet? Oh, forget I said anything."

When I frowned, she added, "Don't fret. It's not anything bad. I just don't want to spoil the surprise."

"If you say so," I replied. I'd had enough surprises to last a lifetime.

She smiled. "I do."

Bianca handed Samantha a key. "Mrs. Wilder has instructed me to give you the key to the room you'll be using to store the decorations. This way, please."

Bianca's midnight-black hair was in a ponytail and it swayed back and forth hypnotically as she led us to a part of the mansion I'd never been to.

We went through rooms even more luxurious than the converted restaurant and ballroom. Sean couldn't keep his astonishment in check and let out a low whistle.

"These are the estate's guest rooms," Bianca said. "It's documented that a famous buccaneer once stayed in one of the bedrooms."

We finally reached stairs much less opulent than the ones near the front entrance. The surroundings grew shabby.

"This part of the house is rarely used," Bianca explained. The wallpaper was faded and torn in places, and I detected the distinct odor of dust and mold, combined with a less familiar smell.

We reached our destination and Bianca motioned for us to enter. We stepped into an enormous room. A row of long narrow windows flanked one wall. At the opposite end, there was a jumble of tables and chairs, and a couple of large trunks. There was even a framed oil painting propped against a dressmaker's dummy. I couldn't decide what to look at next.

I set down the box I'd been carrying. "This is amazing!"

"Well, I'll leave you to it," Bianca said. "Daisy, I'll see you later."

After Bianca left, Samantha said to Sean, "Be an angel and get the folding table first."

"What are you going to do with the folding table?" I asked, after Ryan and Sean left.

"We don't have nearly enough decorations," she replied. "Even with the stuff I've managed to borrow. So, we're going to make more," she said.

"Who is *we?*" I said suspiciously.

"Relax, Daisy," she said. "I've already asked the cheerleading squad to help."

"Great," I said.

"I have bigger plans for you," she said. "I thought you could whip up something for the volunteers to snack on."

"How many volunteers?"

"Just a few," she said airily. "I asked Mrs. Wilder if we could use the kitchen here, but she said her new chef is temperamental."

"I can make some simple stuff," I said.

I had thought I was getting off easily, but my muscles were aching by the time we'd hauled all the supplies to the room. Half of the stuff would have to be moved again when we set up the haunted house.

After we were finished, Ryan took me home, even though Sean lived next door.

"Want to come in?" I was sweaty and tired, but he'd been busy with football practice the last few days and I hadn't seen much of him.

"Nah, I'd better not," he said. He shifted in his seat uncomfortably.

I knew what he was thinking. Despite my best efforts, he and my dad hadn't really clicked.

"Let's go out tomorrow night," I said. "It's Friday."

He gave me a hug. "That sounds great, but I know you want to spend time with your dad."

"I want to spend time with you, too. How about Slim's?"

Slim's Diner was where I worked part-time, but business there had slowed down. Lately I'd only been working the occasional Saturday. It worried me. I didn't know what I'd do if Slim's went out of business. Nightshade wouldn't be Nightshade without the diner.

"Side Effects May Vary is playing at the Black Opal," Ryan said. "But maybe we can hit Slim's after the show."

The front porch light went on, which was my signal to kiss Ryan good night.

When I went inside, my dad was waiting for me. "Where have you been?" he demanded. His hands were shaking.

"Helping Samantha," I said. "Are you okay?"

"Then why did Ryan bring you home?" That's what his agitation was all about.

I drew in my breath. "Ryan was helping, too. And he brought me home because he's my *boyfriend* and he wants to be with me," I said. "You like Ryan, remember?" Dad had never seemed to have a problem with Ryan back when we were little kids who played in the sandbox together, but it was a different story now.

It was hard for me to remember how happy I had been when Mom brought Dad home. Even though I was mad at him, at least it wasn't a doppelganger I was fighting with, which had happened when someone had created doppelgangers of Nightshade residents and tried to pass them off as the real people. This was my real dad and we were having our first real fight.

I stomped up the stairs — ignoring his "Daisy, come back

here!"— and made a beeline for my room, but Poppy waylaid me outside the door.

"What was that all about?" Poppy asked.

"Dad again," I admitted. "I don't know what his problem is with Ryan."

"It's not Ryan," she said. "It's you."

"Huh?" I said. I had no clue what Poppy was talking about.

"Think about it," she said. "You're the baby, and when Dad disappeared, you were twelve."

"I'm following you so far," I said.

"Well, when he came back, he probably still had that image of you in his mind. But you're not twelve anymore. And Ryan just reminds him of that."

"What can I do to make it easier?" I asked.

"Just give him time," she said. "He needs to get used to the idea that you're not his little girl anymore."

"Makes sense," I said. "How'd you get so wise?"

"Psychology 101," she replied. "I love college!"

My two older sisters, Poppy and Rose, both attended UC Nightshade. Poppy had just started her freshman year and Rose was a sophomore.

I retreated to my room, less angry at my dad, but still not in the mood to deal with him. I knew he'd been through a lot, but so had the rest of the family. My mom most of all. And for everyone's sake I needed to try to be more patient with my father.

With that in my mind, I went to find him in the kitchen. "Something smells good," I said.

Dad held up a spoonful of marinara sauce. "Want a taste?"

"Sure," I said. Dad was a great cook, possibly even better than I was.

It was delicious. "Dad, you're the best cook."

Rose came into the kitchen, carrying a pile of mail. She handed me an envelope. "This is for you."

She was still wearing her lab coat. She had a part-time job at a lab on campus. This time, it wasn't working for a mad scientist. She'd worked for her idol Dr. Franken, but that had ended badly when we discovered the professor was in league with the Scourge.

I examined the outside envelope, but it didn't tell me much. I ripped it open and scanned the contents. "It's from the contest I entered this summer," I explained. Natalie, my boss Slim's girlfriend, had convinced me to enter.

"What's it say?" Rose said. "Did you win?"

I read aloud. "We are pleased to inform you . . ." My heart sped up. The grand prize was a trip to Paris, to the famous Cordon Bleu culinary school. "You've won second place."

I stopped reading. Disappointment clogged my throat. I handed the letter to Rose.

"Daisy, this is fabulous!" she said.

"It is?" Had I won after all?

"You've won twelve cooking lessons with a local chef," she said. "And it's Circe Silvertongue."

"Circe Silvertongue?" I said. "She's famous. What's she doing in Nightshade?"

"Didn't you hear?" my dad said. "She's the new head chef at Mrs. Wilder's restaurant." Was that what Bianca was talking about when she mentioned a letter?

"How did you find out?" I asked.

My dad looked away. "It came up when I, er, attended a city council meeting."

Normally a city council meeting would be one of the most boring things imaginable, but this was Nightshade. Nightshade City Council was made up of paranormals, which made for lively meetings. But my dad was a norm, while my mom and sisters and I all had psychic powers. Rose was a telepath, Poppy was telekinetic, and I had a combo pack of powers — part telepathic, part telekinetic, part clairvoyant — but my powers were not exactly reliable.

"Why were you there?" I asked him. I knew the council was anxious to gather information on the Scourge, but I didn't see why they couldn't leave him alone. He hadn't been home that long and was still recovering from his ordeal.

Dad was too thin. Although the shadows in his eyes had faded, they hadn't disappeared entirely. He laid his hand gently on my head. "Don't worry so much," he said. "I volunteered to go. The council just wanted to ask me a few questions about . . . the Scourge."

"Nicholas said the council thinks the Scourge is lying low while they plan something big," Rose chimed in.

Now I was really worried, but I tried not to show it. Rose's boyfriend, Nicholas, was in the know. His dad was the head of the Nightshade City Council. And Nicholas was a werewolf. So was Ryan. Poppy's only serious boyfriend had been a ghost, but Gage had moved on. Literally.

I changed the subject. "It's not the Cordon Bleu, but it sounds pretty cool," I said slowly.

"And it'll look great on your college applications," Rose said.

"College? Already?" Dad said. He sounded a little out of it.

Rose said, "Daisy's a senior, Dad, remember?"

I sent a thought her way. *Is Dad really okay?*

Mom says it'll take time, she sent back.

Mom walked into the kitchen. "How was everybody's day?" she asked cheerfully, but I noticed her eyes flickered anxiously.

"I made dinner," Dad said. He crossed the room to give my mother a lingering kiss.

"Time to set the table," Rose announced loudly, and she and I busied ourselves with cutlery to give them a little privacy. But seeing my parents together, and so obviously still in love, gave me a twinge of hope that everything was going to be all right.

At the dinner table, Mom cleared her throat. "What were you talking about when I came home?" she asked curiously.

"Daisy won cooking lessons with Circe Silvertongue," Rose said quickly. She obviously didn't want to mention Dad's bewilderment to Mom.

"Circe Silvertongue," Mom said. "I'm sure you'll learn a lot from her." But she didn't look happy. When she caught me staring at her, she pasted on a smile, but it didn't take a psychic to figure out that Mom didn't like Circe. I thought about asking her then and there, but Dad looked pale and shaky. He was still sleeping a lot, but had nightmares.

As if he could hear my thoughts, he said, "I think I'll head to bed."

"But you hardly touched your dinner!" Poppy said, then caught herself. We'd agreed we wouldn't hover. "You go ahead," she said, covering her blunder. "I'll clean up."

As soon as Dad was out of sight, dishes began to float off the dining room table and into the kitchen.

"Hey, that's not fair," I said.

"You do it your way, I'll do it mine," Poppy replied. "In fact, you should be practicing with me." She was right. My telekinesis skills weren't getting any better with me just sitting there.

"I'll practice by loading the dishes into the dishwasher," I promised.

"There has to be more for you girls to do with your skills

than household chores," my mother said. "I appreciate the help, but it just seems like —"

"We can't all solve crimes for a living," Rose reminded her. "Although Daisy's getting close to doing it as a serious hobby."

It was true. I'd helped to solve several mysteries in Nightshade, but it had been awfully quiet in the past few weeks.

"Maybe I'll have a nice, safe senior year," I said.

Poppy snorted with laughter. "Or maybe not."

I hated it when my sister was right.

CHAPTER TWO

At school the next day, everyone was talking about the latest addition to Nightshade High. We had a new guidance counselor, Beatrice Tray, who came all the way from Atlanta. She was young, attractive, and Principal Amador thought it was a feather in his cap to have recruited her.

The bell rang, and Ryan and I headed to the cafeteria. We had more classes together this year, but I loved being able to talk to him at lunch, too.

"What happened to Mr. McNamara?" I asked. The old guidance counselor was friendly enough, and I'd grown used to him.

"Someone said he retired suddenly," Ryan told me.

"He was kind of young to retire, wasn't he?" I said.

Ryan shrugged, obviously through talking about it. "Hey, we're still on for tonight, right? I talked to Sean, and he and Samantha are in, too."

"Cool," I said. We were going to an all-ages club, the Black

Opal, to see our favorite local band, Side Effects May Vary. Our school nurse happened to be the bass player.

Ryan grabbed my hand and swung it. "That reminds me," he said. "I have an appointment with her next week."

"With Nurse Phillips?" I said, confused.

"With the new guidance counselor," he said. "It's our senior year, remember? I'm supposed to start narrowing down my college choices."

"How could I forget?" The thought of our possible separation made my good mood disappear. We'd both looked at UC Nightshade, of course, but there was still a very real possibility that Ryan and I might choose colleges far away from each other. It seemed inconceivable that this time next year, I might not see him every day.

"Hey, where'd that smile go?" he said. He pulled me closer, for a hug.

I gave him a tiny smile. It felt forced and he could tell I faked it, but fortunately, the bell rang before I had to explain my sudden bad mood.

The rest of my day didn't improve, but by the time I made it home from school, I had my date with Ryan to look forward to. I was putting the final touches on my makeup when there was a knock on the door.

"Come in," I said.

My dad poked his head in. "Mom's working late," he

said. "But I made your favorite for dinner — peanut butter pancakes."

Breakfast for dinner had been a tradition when I was little. And peanut butter pancakes had been my favorite when I was ten. I repressed a sigh. "Sorry, Dad, but I have a date."

He frowned. "Your mother knows you're going out?"

"Yes, Dad," I said. "She knows."

"Where are you going?"

"To a club," I said.

His frown grew deeper.

Boy, I was really blowing this. "It's an all-ages club and Nicholas works there," I reassured him.

His expression lightened, but I wasn't out of the woods yet. Then the doorbell rang.

Ryan must have picked up on my dad's mood, because my boyfriend's kiss was definitely briefer than usual. My dad cleared his throat and Ryan practically vaulted away from me.

"Hello, Mr. Giordano," Ryan said.

"Ryan," my dad said. We waited for him to say something else. He just stood there, still frowning. "Will you be bringing my daughter home by curfew?"

"I don't really have a curfew," I said, without thinking. I recovered quickly. "But I'm usually home by eleven."

"I'll have her home on time, sir," Ryan assured him.

"Eleven o' clock," Dad barked. "And don't be late."

"Uh, okay. See you later, Dad," I said. I grabbed Ryan's hand

and pulled him out the door. I was trying to understand my dad's point of view, but he was making it difficult. Didn't he trust me? Didn't he trust Ryan? Ryan would never let anything happen to me, at least not while he was still breathing.

"That was intense," Ryan said. "Your dad doesn't like me, does he?"

"It's not you," I replied. "I don't think he would like anyone I was dating."

"You're sure it's not me? Because I'm of the furry persuasion?"

"Positive," I said. "There's no way my father would side with the Scourge in anything." Though he was a norm, my dad was an insider in the paranormal community. His research at UC Nightshade had focused on paranormals, which is why the Scourge kidnapped him.

Ryan nodded and then changed the subject. "Sean and Samantha are meeting us at the club. Samantha had something to do first."

I bet Sam was shopping for a new outfit. I looked down at my jeans and top, suddenly worried that I was underdressed for clubbing.

The parking lot at the Black Opal was already almost full and Side Effects May Vary didn't go on until nine p.m.

As soon as the car stopped, Ryan jumped out and came around to open my door for me. He took my hand as we headed into the club. Nicholas was at the door and he waved to us.

To my surprise, Sean and Samantha were already at a table at the front.

"What took you so long?" she said as we slid into the two empty seats.

"The Inquisition," I said.

"History homework?" Sean asked.

"No, my dad," I replied. "He's still in overprotective mode."

Samantha said, "My dad was like that when I first moved in with him."

Samantha's parents had divorced, and she'd moved in to her dad's place by the university.

"Is he over it yet?"

"Not really," she said. She laughed at my look of gloom. "Cheer up! We have tonight."

Ryan pulled me closer and whispered in my ear. "We have forever."

"I'm surprised you're here so early," I told Samantha. "Ryan said you had something to do first. I thought you'd be picking out a new outfit, or something."

"Those days are long gone, remember? The Devereaux family finances do not allow for splurgy trips to the mall anymore. I just had to pick up a few more supplies for decorations," she explained.

Samantha's family had been rich but had lost their money. She didn't like to talk about it, and I didn't want to pry.

Before I could respond, Side Effects May Vary came

onstage and the room broke out into loud applause. Nurse Phillips was almost unrecognizable in her naughty nurse outfit, teased beehive, and stiletto heels strumming a sparkly turquoise bass guitar. The lead singer wailed out a cover of Billy Idol's "White Wedding."

"C'mon, let's dance," Ryan said.

So we did.

About an hour later, the band took a break and I noticed that Poppy and Rose were at the club, sitting with Nicholas at a table in the back.

Rose and Nicholas were staring into each other's eyes, but Poppy looked completely bored.

I tugged on Ryan's arm. "Let's go say hi to my sisters."

He took my hand and led me through the crowd.

He grabbed two spare chairs and pulled them up to my sisters' table.

"I didn't know you were coming tonight," I said aloud. I sent a message to Rose. *Poppy looks miserable.*

She sent a message back. *I know. I thought a night out would cheer her up.*

Poppy caught on to what we were doing and sent me a scathing look. "Quit doing that," she said. "C'mon, I'm tired of sitting here. I came here to have some fun." She gave one smile to a cute guy with shaggy dark hair standing nearby. He was at our table in a heartbeat, asking her to dance.

Ryan and I followed her and her new friend out on the

23

floor. Even Nicholas and Rose got out of their chairs for a couple of songs.

It seemed like we'd only been there a few minutes, but when I looked at my watch, it was past eleven o'clock.

I'd lost track of the time. "I told Dad I'd be home at eleven," I said.

"Oh, boy," Poppy said. "Are you in trouble."

I stuck out my tongue at her. "I'll call him. I'm sure it will be no big deal."

Nobody picked up, so I relaxed a bit. Dad had probably already gone to bed. Just in case, I left a message. No big deal.

But it was a big deal.

When Ryan and I walked up the walkway, the front door opened and my dad stormed out in his bathrobe.

"Where have you been?" he fumed.

"I told you," I replied. "At the Black Opal."

He pointed to his watch. "You were supposed to be home twenty minutes ago."

"Mr. Giordano," Ryan started to say, but my father interrupted him. "Ryan Mendez, I suggest you head on home yourself. Your father is probably wondering where you are." Then he turned around and stomped inside.

I gave Ryan a very brief kiss and whispered, "I'll be okay. Go ahead and go."

"Are you sure?" he whispered back. "He seems pretty mad."

"I'm positive," I replied.

Dad was waiting for me in the kitchen. He was listening to my message when I came in.

There was a long silence as the sound of my voice faded.

"Daisy, I . . . I'm sorry," he said. "I didn't check the machine and I overreacted."

"Yes, you did," I replied. "But I'm sorry I was late. I wasn't trying to push it, I just —"

"Lost track of time?" he said wryly. "If I would have taken a few more seconds to listen to your message, I would have known that. My apologies. I hope I didn't embarrass you in front of your boyfriend."

"You could never embarrass me," I said. I gave him a hug, and then cleared my throat. "Where's Mom? Still at work?"

Mom was a psychic investigator and often had weird hours. It had been clear early on that Rose and Poppy had inherited her abilities, but everyone had thought I was a normal, just like Dad, until my junior year, when my talents finally manifested.

He nodded. "Yes, but she's due home any minute. She missed dinner so I was just fixing her a salad. Want to help?"

"Sure," I said.

He handed me a head of lettuce and some vegetables and I happily chopped while he whipped up a quick dressing for the salad. It seemed like old times at the Giordano household and I felt a warm glow at having my father back. But he wasn't adapting well to the changes in our lives since he went away. I pushed away the niggling worry that maybe he never would.

CHAPTER THREE

The street fair was the next morning, which was the kickoff to the month-long celebration of Nightshade's two hundredth anniversary.

I was working the information booth with Samantha. She picked me up before I was really awake, and we headed for the fair.

Four blocks of Main Street had been coned off and closed to vehicles. Ryan's dad, Chief Mendez, and another policeman, Officer Denton, were at the entrance, ready to direct the expected traffic.

Our shift didn't start for another half hour, so Sam and I walked along Main Street and watched everyone as they set up their booths. Every store on the street had moved merchandise outside. Slim's and Wilder's both had food booths.

I waved at Slim and Natalie. She was dressed as Catwoman and Slim wore a Batman costume. Most strangers in town would think it was just to play on the Halloween anniversary theme, but I knew it was to disguise the fact that Slim was invisible.

On one side of him was the Donut Hole's booth and the Wilder booth was on the other. The smell of freshly frying donuts filled the air and there was already a line in front of the booth.

My stomach growled and I realized I hadn't eaten breakfast. "C'mon, I'll buy you a donut," I said. I hoped they were serving coffee, too.

"Well, maybe just one," Sam said. "We should bring donuts for the rest of the information booth volunteers, too."

We stood in line and I inhaled the scent of cinnamon, frosting, and grease.

"I wonder if Circe Silvertongue will show up?" I asked Sam.

"I hope so," she said. "The publicity would be fabulous."

Penny Edwards rushed up to us. "I didn't know you two would be here," she said.

"We're the co-chairs," Samantha said.

The what? Uh-oh. That was Sam-speak for *Daisy will be my number-one grunt worker.*

"You are?" Penny said. "I mean, I knew *you* were organizing everything, but I had no idea Daisy was so heavily involved."

Uh, neither did I.

It was finally time to place our order. I ordered a dozen donuts and two coffees. After I paid, I handed Sam her coffee.

"Can I do anything?" Penny asked eagerly.

Sam fished two donuts out of the box and then handed one to me. "Yes," she said. She handed Penny the box. "Take these to the information booth for us."

Penny shot me a dirty look but did as Sam asked. There was a definite flounce to her step as she left.

"That wasn't nice," I said.

Sam shrugged. "She'll be back," she said. "Besides, I wanted to hang with you. I see Penny all the time at cheerleading."

We took our place at the information booth a little while later. I saw Tyler Diaz and a couple of other guys from the basketball team show up. Samantha handed out special T-shirts for the volunteers.

"Sweet, donuts!" said Tyler as he dug into a cruller. "I'm starving."

Penny came up. "Is there anything else I can do?"

"Let me get you a shirt," Sam said.

I felt bad about how we blew her off earlier, so I tried to be nice to her.

"Did you have a donut yet, Penny?" I asked. I handed her a raspberry jelly donut but almost dropped it. As I grabbed it, the jelly squirted out and hit Penny squarely in the face and all over her shirt.

All the guys laughed, except for Tyler.

"You did that on purpose," she hissed.

"It was an accident, I swear. I'm so sorry," I said.

Tyler handed her a paper napkin and she smiled sweetly at him. "Thank you. I'm going to get cleaned up," she said.

"Here," he said. "Take one of these." He handed her a black T-shirt with purple letters that read "What's so normal about Nightshade?" on the front and "Nightshade's Bicentennial, keeping secrets for 200 years" on the back.

"These T-shirts look great, Sam," I said. "I love the calligraphy."

"Penny did the lettering," she said.

A visitor came up to the booth to ask a question and Tyler went to help her.

"I can't believe you, Giordano," Penny said. She wiped the jelly off her face.

"I said I was sorry," I said. Penny seemed unreasonably angry for such a trivial event.

"Sorry isn't good enough," she said. "You better watch it." She made her exit, pushing me a little as she went by me.

"What's her problem?" Sam asked after Penny stormed off.

I shrugged. Her reaction seemed extreme for the situation. Our conversation turned to Samantha's laundry list of things she had to get done for the anniversary celebration.

There was a decent amount of foot traffic for so early in the morning, but after about two hours into our shift, the crowd had grown.

There was a sudden stir of excitement from the crowd. Samantha craned her neck. "It's her!" she said.

29

"Who?" I asked.

A man carrying a television camera on his shoulder stopped at the booth. "Which way to the Wilder's Restaurant booth?" he asked.

Samantha pointed it out and the man hurried off. "Circe Silvertongue is definitely here," she crowed. "This is bound to bring in the tourists."

I was dying to see what she looked liked. I mean, I'd watched her on television, of course, but I wanted to see her in the flesh.

I gave Tyler a pleading look. "Do you mind?"

He chuckled. "You two go ahead," he said. "The guys and I can handle it here for a few minutes."

We joined the excited group surrounding Circe Silvertongue. I recognized her famously patrician features and long silver hair. She wore a designer dress that reached her ankles and a load of heavy silver jewelry, the last of which would not make her popular with some of the locals. Werewolves don't like silver. Only silver bullets could actually kill them, but any silver could do damage.

A local television reporter held a microphone in front of Circe as the camera rolled.

"Yes, I'm thrilled to be in Nightshade," Circe said. She smiled warmly. "I grew up here and returning after so many years is a treat."

"How many years?" The reporter asked.

Circe's smile slipped for a moment, but then she said, "Oh, don't you know it's bad luck to ask a woman her age?"

"Bad luck?" The reporter persisted. "I've never heard that."

"Oh, definitely bad luck." Circe smiled and then changed the subject. "And I have a scoop for you."

"You do?" The reporter was practically drooling, she was so excited.

"I'm pleased to announce that during my tenure as head chef at Wilder's, I will be working on a new cookbook." She was charming.

I nudged Samantha. "I can't believe I won lessons with her!" I said in a low voice. "She seems so nice."

"I know," Sam responded. "I bet her staff looks forward to coming to work every day. I wonder why Mrs. Wilder said she's temperamental."

But the minute the television cameras disappeared, Circe's wide smile disappeared.

"Who is the organizer of this farce?" she snapped.

Samantha stepped forward. "I'm the committee chair," she said bravely. "Is there something I can help you with?"

"My treatment was unacceptable," Circe said. "I wasn't given a bodyguard and I specifically requested Jackal water in the green room."

"We don't have a green room," Samantha said timidly. "In fact, I'm not even sure what a green room is."

Circe snorted. "Of course not." She threw up her hands.

"Why did I ever decide to come back to this backwater?" She looked around with contempt on her face. This is who I would be learning from?

Samantha looked like she was going to cry. I stepped forward, ready to give Circe a piece of my mind. Superstar chef or not, she had no business being rude to my best friend.

Fortunately, just then Mr. Bone arrived on scene, followed closely by Officer Denton. "Circe, you look lovely," he soothed. He took her by the elbow, firmly, I noticed. "Now there are still a few local reporters here," he added. "And I'm sure you'd like to meet with them. Officer Denton will escort you to the area we've set aside for media. In the meantime, I'll procure the water you require."

After Circe was led off by the officer, Mr. Bone patted Samantha on the shoulder. "Don't you worry about Circe Silvertongue," he said. "You're doing an excellent job and the city council is very impressed."

Sam gave him a halfhearted smile. "Circe didn't seem to think so."

"She's a bit high-strung, but I know how to handle her," he replied. "Don't you give her another thought." Mr. Bone bustled off, probably to keep Circe from badmouthing Nightshade.

"He's right, you know," I said to Sam, after he left. "She was just mad because she didn't get the star treatment for once."

But my words had the opposite effect from what I intended.

"She *should* have the star treatment," Sam said gloomily. "I blew it."

We headed back to the information booth, where there was a steady stream of traffic. "The tourists are coming in droves," Tyler said. "Nightshade business owners will be stoked."

Samantha was quiet during the rest of our shift. I could tell that Circe's malicious comments bothered her, but I didn't know what else to say.

When I got home later, Dad seemed like he was waiting for me.

"Hey, how was the street fair?" he asked.

"Great," I said. "You should have come."

He looked down, clearly ashamed. "I get claustrophobic in crowds."

I felt sorry for my dad. I wished that Mom didn't work so much and had more time to keep him company.

"I saw on the news that Circe Silvertongue made an appearance."

"She did," I said. "But she's nothing like we see on TV." Both Dad and I were fans of Circe's show *Cooking with Circe*. Since his return, we had started a new tradition of watching the show together and then cooking the recipes.

"I recorded today's episode," he said. "Wanna watch it?"

"Sure," I replied. "I need some recipe ideas. I told Sam I'd make some snacks for the volunteers."

We settled on the couch with a bowl of popcorn and Dad

clicked on the television. Half an hour later, I found the remote and turned off the recording.

"Wow," I said. "She may not be a very nice person, but she sure can cook."

"So which recipe do you want to make?" Dad said.

"Which one did you like?" I asked.

"I think the white bean dip looked good," he replied. "We can toast pita chips to serve with it. Or the wonton cups with cream cheese."

"Then let's make both!" I said. I spent the evening cooking with my dad. Seeing him in the kitchen, laughing and joking, made me feel like the years he was missing had never happened.

CHAPTER FOUR

Monday morning, I grabbed my binder and then slammed my locker shut. I hoped I hadn't forgotten my homework at home, but nothing would surprise me. I wasn't looking forward to my cooking lessons with the famous Circe Silvertongue. At least, not after how she acted at the street fair.

"Can you believe that scene at the fair?" I asked Sam. "Circe was so nasty." The chef's behavior had bugged me the rest of the weekend, but I'd tried to tell myself she'd been in a bad mood when we saw her.

"She was intense," Sam agreed. "But she has to be nice to you. You're the contest winner."

"Maybe," I said, but I wasn't hopeful.

"She came into Tete de Mort on Sunday," Sam confided. "She bought a purse."

"That's nice," I said.

Samantha laughed. "I know you don't care that much about fashion, but even you have to be impressed. She bought a one-of-a-kind La Contessa, which cost over five thousand dollars."

"For a purse? That's obscene."

"Obscene or not, I get the commission," Samantha said. She did a little dance.

"That's fantastic," I said. "What are you going to do with the money?"

"College fund," she replied, and then changed the subject. "Want to help out tonight? Craft session at the Wilders'."

"Sure," I said. "I need to find out about scheduling my cooking lessons, anyway."

I stopped at home after school to pick up the snacks I had made, and Samantha came by and picked me up in her little red VW convertible. Rachel and Jordan were in the back seat. As I slid into the front seat, I noticed my dad was staring out the window at us, an anxious look on his face.

I sighed.

Sam noticed my dad, too. She gave him a merry little wave and he returned it. "How is he?" she asked me.

"Better," I said. "But he's driving me crazy. I thought when he came home, everything would be perfect, but he . . ."

"Hovers?"

"Exactly," I said. "He's way overprotective."

Jordan said, "It must be weird for him, you know."

Sam looked at her in the rearview mirror. "What do you mean?"

"Can you imagine?" Jordan replied. "Locked up all that time. He probably thought about his family every single day, picturing you the way you were the last time he saw you. And then he finally gets home and everything has changed."

"You're right," I said. Jordan and I weren't close, but she and Sam were. Her compassion for my father made me realize what Sam saw in her.

After that, the conversation turned to more general things. "How's the squad?" I said, a tiny bit wistfully. I'd been a cheerleader for about ten minutes last year, and a part of me missed it.

Rachel smiled at me. "You'll get a chance to see for yourself," she said. "Sam convinced everyone to lend a hand with the anniversary celebration."

"I'll bet she did," I kidded.

Even Samantha laughed.

After we reached the long driveway leading to the Wilder estate, I said, "Can you let me off here? I'll meet you in the workroom as soon as I'm done talking to Circe."

I cut through the garden but was careful to stick to the main path. The Wilders were shifters and you never knew who or what you'd run in to on their property if you weren't careful. I suppressed a shudder as I passed the topiary maze. Bad memories.

Wilder's Restaurant wasn't open yet, but the French doors, the ones with the view of the maze, were flung wide to let in the fresh air. Delicious smells wafted through the deserted restaurant.

I stopped to speak to a young woman in a severe black uniform with a starched white shirt setting the tables.

"Hi. Could you tell me where I might find Circe Silvertongue?"

"It's your funeral," she said wryly.

At my startled look, she continued. "Oh, forget I said that. Circe is just . . . having a rough day," she clarified, obviously choosing her words carefully.

Great. I was stuck with a high-maintenance chef. Still, free cooking lessons were free cooking lessons.

I followed my nose to the enormous back kitchen. It was empty, which was rather unusual at this time of day. There ought to be assistant chefs, a sous-chef, prep workers, bustling around, preparing for the dinner rush.

I heard raised voices and I followed the sound to a small office tucked away at the rear of the kitchen.

"I insist you stop this now," Bianca hissed.

"And I am telling you, I will not," Circe replied. "It seems as though we are at an impasse."

"If Mrs. Wilder finds out —" But whatever else Bianca was going to say stopped when she caught sight of me.

"Daisy," she said. "What are you doing here?" Not exactly the warm welcome I'd hoped for.

"The letter," I explained. I was sure I wasn't imagining it; a strange look passed between Circe and Bianca.

"What letter?" Circe said sharply.

"The contest," I clarified. "Cooking lessons."

"Oh, yes, that," Circe said. She didn't sound exactly enthused. In fact, she sounded relieved.

"I was dying to tell you that you had won the cooking lessons last time you were here," Bianca said.

I glanced at Circe's desk, curious to see if she had already started working on the cookbook she'd mentioned. I would have loved to see a new recipe, but all I saw was one of those heavy-looking expensive pens. This one was black with silver initials, engraved *B* and *M*, along the widest part.

Circe caught me looking at it. "Nice, isn't it?" she said. "I handwrite the menus every day. This is my favorite pen."

"You handwrite the menus?" I said, imagining all the work that that must entail.

"Just the specialty list," she said. "I think it adds an elegant touch."

I surveyed the rest of her office, awed in spite of myself. There were photos hanging of her with the mayor of New York, the governor of California, and even Bono. I also saw a heavily embossed envelope with a red wax seal. It looked just like the one Wolfgang had. Why would Wolfgang and Circe get the same letter?

"Now, about your cooking lessons . . ." Circe's voice interrupted my train of thought.

Before we could start, however, a cold nose pressed into the back of my leg. A strange snuffling noise came from that general direction.

I looked down. There was a pig in the kitchen. A large potbellied pig, with a cold snout and wiry hair sprouting on its head. It looked almost like it had a head of hair.

"Bad baby," Circe cooed. "You scared our guest."

The pig snorted. Big brown eyes looked up at me pleadingly.

Circe's tone turned to ice. "How many times have I told you that you will behave in my kitchen? If you don't behave, I'm going to have to punish you."

The words sent a shiver through the pig and then it turned and trotted off.

"She seems to be well trained," I finally said.

"He," Circe corrected me. "His name is Balthazar. Trufflehunting pigs are usually female, but I have one of the few males."

Circe stared after her pig for a long moment before she finally remembered I was still standing there.

"Now then," she said. "Let's get started."

We went over my experience and she seemed impressed that I'd been doing some of the cooking at Slim's. "Excellent," she said. "When would you like to start?"

We worked out a schedule, and then she said, "You're sure your employer won't mind?"

Without thinking, I replied, "Oh, no, it's been slow there."

I didn't imagine Circe's look of satisfaction.

Bianca frowned at her. I did, too. If Circe thought she'd get one more bit of information about Slim's from me, she was dead wrong.

"I've got to go," I said. "But I'll be here on Saturday."

The lessons were going to be twice a week, and I was wondering how I was going to be able to fit it into my already busy schedule.

"I don't know how you do it," I said to Sam, once I'd rejoined her and the rest of the volunteers in the storage room.

"What do you mean?" she asked.

"I mean, you manage to do it all," I said. "Cheerleading, student council, working at the boutique, heading this committee . . ."

She leaned in. "I'll tell you my secret," she said, pausing dramatically.

"I'm listening."

"There are really two of me," she said.

"Not even funny," I said. And it wasn't. Nightshade had had an influx of doppelgangers not that long ago, and it hadn't been a pleasant experience.

Her grin faded. "Daisy, I'm so sorry!" she said. "I completely forgot."

I smiled at her reassuringly. "Maybe that's a good thing," I replied.

I waved to Lilah Porter, who was working on a mural. I went over to check it out.

"This is amazing," I said to her. It was a fantastic ocean scene of Nightshade, complete with sailors, mythical beasts, and singing mermaids.

"Thanks," she said. "It's for the ballroom. What are you working on?"

"I'm afraid I don't have your talent," I said. "Strictly coloring in the lines." I held up a half-finished papier-mâché bat.

"How many of these things did you say we needed?" I asked Sam.

"I didn't," she said. "I was afraid it would freak you out. We still have to make papier-mâché pumpkins and cats."

I sighed. It was going to be a long night.

Eventually, people started to leave. I yawned and stretched. It was getting late and I had glue in my hair and black paint all over my hands. I wanted some food and a shower, in that order.

Sam, Jordan, Rachel, and I were the only people left when a strange rustling noise was heard coming from the other end of the room.

"Do you think it's a rat?" Rachel asked.

"Let's take a look," Jordan said.

"I'll pass on the bubonic plague," Samantha drawled. I stayed with her, just to keep her company, of course.

When Rachel and Jordan went to investigate, Jordan accidentally knocked something over. It was the painting I had noticed the first day I went to the room. It had been propped in the corner, turned away from view. We gasped as it clattered to the ground, but it landed face-up. She turned it over and examined it. "It's okay," she said with relief.

"Bianca told us to stay away from that stuff," Samantha warned, but they ignored her.

"What is that?" Rachel said.

"It's a painting of a young woman," Jordan said. "She's beautiful."

Sam and I looked at each other and then trooped over to take a look. We couldn't help it.

She *was* beautiful, but there was something spooky about her. Her long dark hair was parted in the middle and swept up into a bun and a locket hung around her neck. There was a faint frown on her face. On the back, in faded handwriting, there was one word. Lily.

The rustling came again and we all jumped. "What was that?" Samantha said.

"Maybe it's a mouse," I said, but I was getting a strange vibe. I felt *someone* was listening in on our conversation.

The sound came closer.

Samantha and Jordan were holding on to each other, but Rachel had picked up a folding chair, ready to swing it. I admired Rachel's spunk. I was preparing to use my power of telekinesis when Bianca came into view.

We all breathed sighs of relief.

"Is everything all right?" she said.

"We . . . You startled us, that's all," I said.

"Mrs. Wilder has asked that I close up for the day," Bianca continued. "Wilder's will be closed to the public tonight. A . . . private event."

It was clear that they wanted us out of their hair, so we packed up and called it a night.

The rest of the week passed without incident, except for a pop quiz in calculus on Wednesday, which I was prepared for. Sam caught up with me after my last class. Sean and Ryan had lockers right next to ours.

"Do you need a ride home?" Sam asked. "I'm taking Katie shopping after school." Katie was Sean's sister. Samantha spent nearly as much time with Sean's family as she did with Sean. I think she was lonely sometimes. Even though Mrs. Devereaux wasn't the greatest mom in the world, I knew Sam missed her. She'd moved to San Francisco after the divorce and rarely visited.

"Ryan is coming over, so I'm set, thanks." My father had a job interview at some college a couple of hours away. It was a non-tenured position and the salary was a lot less than he used to make, but he was excited about the interview. He had a friend on the faculty there and would be out of the house until late.

I glanced over at my boyfriend, who had an expression that

told me he'd completely forgotten our plans.

"Daisy, I have an appointment with Ms. Tray after school today," he confessed.

I tried not to let my feelings show. Ryan hated disappointing me and I didn't want to make him feel any worse than he obviously did.

"It's okay," I said. "I'll get a ride home with Sam. Maybe you can come over later?"

"I'd love to," he said. "But I don't know how late I'll be."

"Come over whenever," I said. "After his interview, Dad's having dinner out."

"What's the matter, Ryan?" Sean teased. "Scared of the old man?"

"Cut it out, Sean," he replied. "I'm not scared. Just cautious." When I laid a hand on his arm, he gave me a look meant to reassure me. But it didn't.

I caught a ride home with Samantha.

"How are plans for Merriweather House coming along?" I asked.

"I may have bitten off more than I can chew," Samantha admitted. "I might need more of your help than I first thought."

"Of course!" Samantha didn't admit to needing help very often. Usually, she commandeered volunteers and made it look like she was doing them a favor.

When I got home, I made a quick batch of chocolate chip

cookies and slid them in the oven, then sat at the kitchen counter, waiting for Ryan to show. When he came to the door, I was pleased to see that he wasn't *that* late. He stood on my front porch and I had to restrain myself from touching the curls at the nape of his neck.

We went to the kitchen and I offered him a freshly baked cookie. He took one and ate it absent-mindedly.

"I had the best meeting with the new counselor," Ryan said. We had the house to ourselves, but he didn't have romance on his mind. He was all amped up after his meeting.

"She said that I should apply to a couple of out-of-state schools." My normally laid-back boyfriend was practically bouncing in his chair with excitement.

"Out-of-state?" I was careful to keep the alarm I felt from my voice.

Ryan and I had been talking about UC Nightshade. I didn't want to be too far from home, since Dad had just returned. And Ryan thought that UC Nightshade would be werewolf friendly.

A thought struck me. "You didn't tell her about your condition, did you?"

"No, of course not," Ryan said. "But I don't think she'd care. Ms. Tray thinks I have a lot of potential."

I don't know exactly why this was making me so miserable. I should be happy that Ryan had someone to help him with his options for college.

"She's super nice," he continued. "She wants to meet you, too."

"She does?" I said. "Why?"

"To find out more about you," he said. "To help you the way she's helping me."

"Er, great," I said. Ryan didn't even notice the lack of enthusiasm in my voice.

"I can't wait to tell my dad about the meeting. Do you mind? I'd love to try to catch him before he gets called out or goes to bed or something."

I sighed. "Of course not."

I said good night to my boyfriend and then went into the living room to watch a little television. Not exactly the way I envisioned my evening. I must have dozed off, because the next thing I knew, I heard a car door slam.

I knew it was late because Letterman was on. I clicked off the TV and then Dad appeared in the doorway.

"Where is everyone?" he said.

"Mom and Poppy are both still working and Rose is out with Nicholas," I said. I smothered a yawn. Poppy had a new job this fall at the campus coffee shop.

"Oh." He hovered in the doorway. "I guess I'll go to bed, then."

"Me, too." I yawned again.

Instead of heading upstairs, he stood there uncertainly.

I remembered Rose's advice to include Dad in my life.

"Dad, Nightshade High is having a fundraiser next weekend," I said. "Do you want to come?"

He smiled. "I'd love to," he said. "Your mother and I haven't been to a school event in . . . years." His smile faltered, but I pretended not to notice.

I felt a twinge at the thought that all it took to make him happy was a little bit of my life.

"You can meet our principal, Mr. Amador," I said.

"Sounds great," he said.

"And maybe afterward, we can all go to Slim's. I can show you where I work."

I'd said something wrong. His face closed up. "I wish you didn't have to work."

"I don't *have* to work, Dad," I said. "I want to." Which was mostly true.

I said good night and headed for my room, but I couldn't sleep. Dad was still struggling with his treatment at the hands of the Scourge and it was coming out in weird ways.

CHAPTER FIVE

Dad was still being all weird and wouldn't let me go to San Carlos for the away game on Thursday night. Practically the whole town, including my boyfriend, would be at that game, except for me. I was feeling sorry for myself when Poppy came home from class. I convinced her to come with me to Slim's Diner.

"Isn't it kind of lame to go to the place you work?" Poppy said.

"Dad won't let me go to the game," I said. "And what else is there to do in Nightshade?"

Slim's was a true diner, with red leather booths, shiny chrome counters, and an old-fashioned jukebox in the corner. But it was definitely not like other jukeboxes. She (because I was sure the jukebox was female, I'd even named her Lil) played what she wanted, when she wanted. Sometimes, when she was really mad at me, she wouldn't play at all.

The place was packed with tourists. I didn't recognize a

single face there except Flo's. Poppy and I sat at the counter. That was the only place left to sit.

Slim had created a special menu for the paranormal tourists. I tried not to think too hard about what exactly was in blood soup, although Slim assured me it was goose blood.

Flo bustled up to us a few minutes later. Her T-shirt read "The rumors are true." Flo had an endless collection of snarky T-shirts, several tattoos, and a serious attitude. Her real name was Florence. Only her brother Slim called her that and lived to tell the tale.

"Hi, Flo," I said. "How are things?"

"I'm in the weeds," she admitted. "What can I get you?"

"I'll help," I said. I hopped down from the stool and grabbed an apron from behind the counter in an attempt to save my outfit. "What do you need me to do first?"

"I hate to ask, but would you mind cooking?" Flo replied.

"Where's Slim?" I asked.

"He went to get some supplies for the dinner rush," Flo replied. "We've been getting a lot of requests for items off the special menu."

"Oh," I said, suddenly understanding. I scanned the crowd and recognized that 90 percent of the tourists were of the supernatural variety. It wasn't obvious at first, but I'd lived in Nightshade long enough to know when pale skin meant a lethal allergy to daylight and when a thick hairy neck meant more than a need for a trip to the barbershop.

An elderly vamp kept eyeing my neck like it was a particularly tasty treat. Which, in a way, I guess it was. At least for vampires. His gaze made me wish I'd worn something a little less revealing, like a parka and a few dozen scarves.

Poppy brought water glasses to the tables while Flo took orders. I ran to the back and took a quick survey of what supplies I had on hand to work with. There was just enough raw meat for the steak tartare the Were family had ordered, but the vampires would have to make do with duck-blood soup, instead of goose.

I wasn't sure, but I thought the hags in the corner booth might like the frogs' legs, so I got those out, too.

As the orders poured in, I cheated a bit and used my telekinesis to chop, stir, and flip when I didn't think anyone was watching. Supernatural or not, there were a lot of out-of-towners in the crowd.

"Daisy, you're a lifesaver," a voice said in my ear. "I've got it from here. Thanks!" A spatula hovered in the air for a second, and then rapidly flipped the patties cooking on the grill.

My boss was back. He was invisible, so it wasn't always easy to tell. Slim continued. "Go enjoy what's left of your night." The spatula gestured to the front door, where Sean, Samantha, and Ryan stood.

The majority of the crowd had been fed, so I went over to talk to them.

"What are you doing here?"

Ryan said, "I was looking for you."

My boyfriend was the greatest. "I'm glad you found me."

"I didn't know you were working tonight," Sam said.

"Neither did I," I replied. I gestured to the full restaurant. "Poppy and I came in for dinner, but the place was slammed." I looked around for her and saw she was at the cash register.

"Let's grab that booth," Ryan said. The Were family was leaving, so I cleared the tabletop and Poppy came over with a cloth and wiped it off and we sat down.

"I'm starving," Sean said.

Then I remembered something. "Hey, why aren't you guys wearing your jerseys?" The football team always wore jerseys on game day. "And Samantha's not in her cheerleading uniform, either. What happened to the game tonight?"

Ryan shook his head. "Game was canceled."

"Why?" Poppy said. "I can't remember the last time a football game between Nightshade and San Carlos was canceled."

"Something happened at the other school," Sean said.

"Something bad? At San Carlos?"

"We got all the way there," Ryan replied. "And they just called off the game. And they're not saying why."

"Weird," I said.

Poppy hesitated when Flo came to take our order. "Maybe I'll just head home," she said.

I didn't need my psychic abilities to tell that Poppy was feeling like a third (or was it fifth?) wheel.

"Please stay," Ryan said. "I wanted to hear about the classes you're taking at UC Nightshade. Daisy and I are both talking about going there."

I squeezed his hand under the table. I loved that he was trying to put my sister at ease. And I loved that he hadn't given up on UC Nightshade.

"I guess I could stay for a little bit," Poppy said.

"And dinner is on the house," my boss called out.

"Slim, you don't have to do that," I replied.

"I insist."

We chatted about the campus and Poppy's favorite professors until the meal came.

A familiar-looking cute guy walked in and stood at the cash register. He had dark hair that fell to his collar, and his eyes were such a dark brown that they looked almost black.

I nudged Poppy. "Is that the guy you were dancing with at the Black Opal?" I asked.

She glanced over at him. He caught her looking and smiled, but she turned her attention back to her food. "I don't know. He's just some guy."

Which meant, in Poppy-speak, "not Gage." Still, the guy in question was hot, no doubt about it.

It seemed like he might work up the courage to come over and say hi, but he lost his nerve at the last minute. Flo walked over carrying a large to-go container. He took his food, paid the bill, and after one last longing look at Poppy, he left.

Flo brought us more food than we had ordered, including enormous chocolate shakes. Everything was delicious, but Poppy only picked at her salad and didn't even touch her shake. I don't know how she could pass it up. Slim's had the best food in town.

I had something I wanted to ask Sean. "Hey, Sean, did Wolfie ever mention what was in that envelope?"

He stopped mid-chew, clearly not understanding the question. He swallowed and then said, "Oh, you mean the letter that fell out of his bag?"

I nodded.

"Nah," he replied. "But Wolfie was awfully mad that I took his bag by mistake."

"Madder than usual?"

Sean shrugged. "It's kind of hard to tell."

It was true. Wolfie was always a little surly. He came from a shifter family, but he had a chip on his shoulder.

"Daisy, can I talk to you for a minute?" Flo said. She sent the gang a quick look. "In private?"

"Sure," I said. I followed her into the back.

She went to the office, where she pulled an envelope from the mail cubby and held it up. "This came today."

She handed it to me and I turned it over. Someone had opened it at the top with a letter opener, which left the red seal intact. There was something ominous about that red seal. The red wax had dripped, leaving little spots on the creamy white paper. It looked like drops of blood.

"Go ahead, read it," she said.

I took it gingerly and unfolded the note. *I know what you are* was written in fancy calligraphy on the stationery.

"That's it?"

"Isn't that enough?" she said. "It came for Slim, but I opened it. I know how you love a good mystery, so I thought you might be interested."

Wolfgang's letter looked just like this one. I wondered if it said the same thing.

"Strange," I said. "I'll keep my eyes open, but I don't know what it means."

"I do," she said. "It means someone is trying to blackmail us."

"They don't ask for anything," I pointed out.

"Not yet," she said. "But trust me, they will."

"I'll ask my sisters and the gang to keep their eyes and ears open," I said. "If that's all right."

"Yes, but please be discreet," she said. "Slim has enough problems right now."

I promised Flo I'd do what I could to help and then went

back to the front. I thought maybe Lil would give me a little help. I put the quarters in and punched in my selection, but the jukebox stubbornly refused to play. I tried again. Still nothing. If Lil knew anything, she certainly wasn't talking.

I shrugged. "Sorry." I was talking to myself, but the jukebox must have thought my apology was meant for her because "Happy" by Leona Lewis blasted out a second later.

The sound cut off abruptly when Circe Silvertongue entered the restaurant.

Flo was sitting at her favorite stool at the counter, but she didn't move when Circe walked up.

"A little service here," Circe demanded.

Flo stomped over to our table and refilled our water glasses. "What's she doing here?" she hissed.

Circe stood at the cash register, waiting, but Flo pointedly ignored her until Slim said, "Florence," in a no-nonsense voice.

Flo then stomped her way over to the register. "Can I help you?"

Circe ignored Flo's scowl. "I placed an order to go," she said.

"The famous chef is eating at our diner. We're honored," Flo said, but her words didn't match her tone.

"Everyone gets tired of their own cuisine," Circe replied.

Flo snorted, and the little bell in front of the chef's window began to ding wildly. "Order up, Florence," Slim said. "Now!" he added when it looked like Flo was going to say something snide to Circe.

"What's that all about?" Ryan asked.

"I guess Flo doesn't like Circe," I said.

"Well, tell us something we don't know," Samantha said. "The question is *why* doesn't Flo like her?"

"I have no idea." But Circe gave us a clue a second later.

"How much for the jukebox?" Circe said.

"A quarter per song," Flo replied.

"I mean how much to buy the jukebox."

Flo looked like she was actually considering it.

"I will pay you top dollar for her," Circe said. "This place is just holding on by a thread. You obviously need the money."

For her? How did Circe know that Lil was female?

"The jukebox is not for sale," I interjected. I sent Flo a pleading look.

Circe's eyes gleamed green, which seemed like a bad sign. "This does not concern you, Daisy."

"You can't buy the jukebox," I said.

Flo put a hand on my arm. "Go spend time with your friends," she said curtly. "I'll deal with Circe." The tattoo on her bicep swirled, I was sure of it.

"Please don't sell Lil," I said.

"Circe collects things, Daisy," Flo said. "I'd hate for you to become one of her pets."

"There's no chance of that," I said. "I'm not anyone's pet."

I did what she asked and went back to the table. When I looked up, Circe was gone.

But the jukebox was still there, and for that I was grateful.

Without warning, Lil launched into "Bad Woman" by the Arctic Monkeys.

I agreed with her completely. Lil had always been there for me. I'd buy the jukebox myself before I let Circe have her. Somehow.

CHAPTER SIX

Samantha and I were scheduled to head to the haunted house location after school on Friday. I grabbed the Tupperware containers of the snacks I'd made for the volunteers and met her in the parking lot. I helped Sam load a cooler full of sodas and waters into her car, and we were on our way.

I'd seen the abandoned mansion before, of course, but from a distance. I was really curious. It wasn't far from the Wilder estate, Merriweather House couldn't be seen from the main road.

The driveway was pockmarked with ruts and Sam decided to park a way down the lane and walk. Her peppy little VW convertible wasn't meant for four-wheeling.

"Just wait until you see it," Samantha said. "You're just going to die!"

We rounded the bend and the house came into view. I suppressed a gasp.

"It's criminal that someone let a house as beautiful as this go."

"The structure is still sound," Sam assured me. "Mrs. Wilder wouldn't agree to let us use it until she had it inspected."

"Mrs. Wilder owns this house, too?" Merriweather House was almost as large as the Wilder place.

Sam shrugged. "I dunno," she said. "All I know is it has something to do with her sister."

There were several women from Mom's garden club scrubbing down the front hallway. I didn't expect my grandma to be one of them. My normally elegant grandmother wore faded bib overalls, the same bright purple T-shirt as the other volunteers, and her hair was protected by a matching purple scarf.

"Daisy!" Grandma Giordano said. "I'm so glad you're getting into the volunteer spirit."

"Hi, Grandma," I said. "I didn't expect to see you here. You remember my friend Samantha?"

"Of course," Grandma Giordano said. "How are you, my dear?"

"Fine, thanks," Sam said. "I really appreciate you helping out."

"Where should we set up the snacks?" I said.

"We've already cleaned most of the front parlor," my grandmother said.

"Perfect," Samantha said. She grabbed the cooler and led the way.

The front parlor was full of heavy wood furniture, a red velvet sofa, and a sea of purple T-shirts.

"I finally thought of a theme for the ball," Samantha said excitedly. "A typical Halloween costume party might be . . . tricky in Nightshade."

"So what did you come up with?" I asked her.

"Nightshade through the ages. It's going to be a costume ball, but everyone has to dress up as someone from Nightshade's history."

"That's a great idea," I said, already worrying about what I would wear.

Samantha picked up immediately on my anxiety. "Don't worry," she said. "I'll help you find something great to wear to the ball."

"Thanks," I said. "You know I rely on you for fashion advice."

"I'm thinking vintage," she replied. "Same for this place. Each room off the ballroom will represent a different era. We'll make this the Victorian room."

"Cool idea," I said. "I'm going to work with my grandmother for a while, if that's okay?"

"Sure," she said. "I need to check out the progress in the ballroom."

After Sam left, Grandma handed me a soft cloth and furniture polish.

"We've cleaned the floors and the walls," she said. "Now we need to tackle the furniture."

"This house is in pretty good shape," I commented to Grandma.

"Mrs. Wilder hired a caretaker several years ago," Grandma said. "He keeps an eye on the place and does the major repairs."

"Why would she do that?" I asked, curious.

"Haven't you heard the story?" Grandma said. "Well, I guess it was way before your time. Mrs. Wilder's sister, Lily, was engaged to the fellow who owned Merriweather House."

Lily . . . Why did that name ring a bell? I remembered the portrait I'd seen at the Wilders'. "What happened?"

"Her sister disappeared the night they announced their engagement."

"What happened to the fiancé?" I asked.

"Nobody knows," Grandma said. "At first, everyone thought they'd eloped, but when no one heard from them, the family hired a private detective. The detective never found them." She pointed to a portrait hanging over the mantel. "That's him there."

I crossed the room for a better look. The portrait was covered in dust. I carefully wiped it away with a soft cloth. "He's handsome," I said.

"Bam Merriweather had the reputation as quite the lady's man until he met Lily," Grandma said.

"What kind of a name is Bam?" I wondered.

Grandma shrugged. "A nickname, I'm sure," she said. "Now that I think about it, I never heard him called by his given name."

"What was Lily's last name? Mrs. Wilder's maiden name?"

"Varcol, I think," she said. "They were head over heels in

love. He broke quite a few hearts when the engagement was announced."

"And I always thought that Mrs. Wilder must have the best life," I said.

"Just because she is wealthy doesn't mean she's had it easy," Grandma rebuked me gently.

"Do you remember anything else?" I asked.

Grandma shook her head.

"I wish I could help," I said impulsively.

"After all this time, I don't know if it's wise to open old wounds," she said.

"Maybe," I said. "But if your sister disappeared, wouldn't you want to know what happened? Even after all this time?"

Grandma admitted, "If it were me, I'd want to know, no matter how many years had passed."

We cleaned in silence, but I couldn't get my mind off the tragic story. I decided to go find Samantha and let her know I wanted to snoop around a bit.

"Grandma, which way is the ballroom?" I asked.

"Down that hall," she said, pointing to the left. "But the second and third floors are off-limits."

But when I passed a staircase, I noticed a blond woman in a purple T-shirt on the second floor. There was something surreptitious about the way she moved along the galley.

"Excuse me," I said to her, but she ignored me and kept moving.

I paused indecisively. Should I go after her or get Sam? The woman returned a few minutes later and started down the stairs.

"We're not supposed to be on the upper floors," I called out to her.

Samantha walked in as I was confronting the stranger. "Daisy, I see you've met Ms. Tray," she said.

I gaped at her. "Ms. Tray?"

"Our new guidance counselor," she said.

"Oh, I'm sorry I yelled at you," I finally said. "But I was told we aren't supposed to be on the second floor."

"Darlin'," she said, with a thick southern accent. "You must be mistaken. I wasn't on the second floor."

She looked at me like I was completely crazy. If it wasn't her, then who could it have been? Had I seen a ghost? Then I noticed the footprints in the dusty stairs. She *had* been upstairs. I wasn't crazy.

We continued our conversation, but my brain was busily dealing with the fact that the new guidance counselor had lied, right to my face.

CHAPTER SEVEN

My first cooking lesson did not go well.
First of all, I was ten minutes late. Poppy had disappeared with
the car and there was nobody else home, not even Dad. Finally,
in desperation, I noticed that Sean's car was in his driveway and
rang his doorbell.

"I need a big favor," I said. His little sister Katie peeked out
from behind him.

Five minutes later, Katie, Sean, and I were on our way to
the Wilder estate.

"I really appreciate this," I said to Sean. Katie was playing
with a hand-held video game in the back seat.

"No problem," he said. "But I don't actually have to see that
Circe woman, do I? She freaks me out."

"No, she'll be in the kitchen," I assured him. "But why does
she freak you out?"

"I've heard stories," Sean said. "There's this friend of my
dad's who used to work for her cooking show. He says she plays
dirty."

"What did he mean by that?" I asked.

Sean shrugged. "Not sure, but I wouldn't trust her if I were you, Daisy."

He dropped me off at the front and then took off slowly. I'd never noticed before, but Sean drove very carefully when his little sister was in the car.

I also noticed Penny Edwards, hunched down in the front seat of her parked car and glaring at me. I figured she must be here to work on decorations with Sam and the rest of the volunteers. I wondered why she was giving me such a dirty look. Could she still be mad about the jelly donut incident last week?

I didn't have time to ponder Penny's problem for long. I looked at my watch and took a shortcut through the garden steering clear of the maze. It still gave me the creeps, even in the daylight.

I entered the kitchen, out of breath.

"You are late," Circe said. She didn't look up from her mixing bowl.

Did someone leave the refrigerator door open? Because there was definitely cold air blowing from somewhere.

"I'm sorry," I said. "My sister took the car and . . ."

She finally looked up. Her eyes were glowing green. Witchy eyes. I sensed danger, but I couldn't look away.

"It won't happen again," she stated.

"It won't happen again," I parroted. I tried to move, but I was frozen there.

She smiled. "Good."

The ice in my spine dissipated and I was able to move. I took one faltering step and then another until I reached her side.

"What are you working on?" My mouth felt stiff as I spoke.

"A new truffle sauce recipe," she replied.

Personally, I thought truffles smelled like old socks soaked in vinegar, but they seemed to be popular with the customers at Wilder's.

Still, the idea was to learn a little more sophisticated method of cooking, so I kept quiet about my doubts and watched her carefully.

She took something out of her pocket and sprinkled it into the pan. A strange aroma filled the kitchen.

"Is that a new herb?" I asked her. "I've never smelled anything like it before."

"It's . . . my own blend," she said. "A Circe Silvertongue secret."

That was a secret she could keep. It smelled horrible. At least at first. A few minutes later, the smell of the sauce bubbling on the stove was making my mouth water.

"Can I have a taste?" I said eagerly.

She gave me a long measuring look. "Not yet," she decided. "Maybe someday."

She went to the walk-in refrigerator and returned with a small container of white rice. She scooped some of the rice into a doggie bowl and then poured the sauce over it.

"Balthazar," she cooed. "Mommy has something for you."

Balthazar ran up and ate his meal eagerly. When he had finished, he went obediently back to Circe's office.

The rest of my "cooking" lesson consisted of me scrubbing the pots and pans she'd left soaking in the sink. I thought about protesting, but one look from Circe's green eyes changed my mind.

When I was finally finished, I texted Poppy to pick me up "or else" and waited in the break room. About ten minutes later, she sent me a message that she was in the Wilder's parking lot.

It was dark, but I cut through the patio anyway. The restaurant was empty of customers, but the French doors were still open. I heard Bianca's raised voice and stopped.

"You can't do this," she said. "I won't let you."

"You can't stop me," Circe replied. "I can't let the information . . ."

They moved out of my hearing. I tried some psychic eavesdropping, but I didn't pick up anything else, except that one of the busboys had a crush on Samantha. Big surprise. So did half the senior class.

I walked to the parking lot, wondering the whole time what Circe and Bianca were arguing about.

When I got in the car, Poppy rolled the windows down. "You smell like you've been rolling in a pig pen," she said.

"I've been working," I said. She could be such a pain in the butt sometimes. The next minute, she made up for it. She handed me a big cup of coffee.

"You are the best sister in the world," I declared. I sipped it and then told Poppy about the weird experience I'd had with Circe.

"She has a pet pig?" Poppy asked.

"That's not the weird part." I told her about the blast of icy air and feeling rooted to the spot.

"Do you think she's a witch?" she asked.

"Not exactly," I replied. "But she's definitely *something*."

She agreed with me, but we couldn't come up with any ideas.

We had just walked in the door of our house and I was ready to relax, when my cell rang. It was Samantha.

"What are you doing tonight?" she asked.

"Why do you want to know?" I replied suspiciously. I was in no mood to be roped into volunteering after the long day I'd had with Circe, but that didn't mean anything. Not when it was Sam I was talking to.

"Jordan's having a slumber party," she explained. "And you're invited."

"A slumber party?" I said doubtfully.

"C'mon, it'll be fun," she said. "All the cheerleaders will be there."

Fortunately, a slumber party sounded sufficiently juvenile to satisfy my father and he said I could go.

Twenty minutes later, Sam honked her horn and I grabbed my stuff and headed out.

"What's in the grocery bag?" she asked.

"I thought we could make s'mores," I said. "Unless you think that's lame?"

"It's perfect," Sam assured me. "Jordan wants to build a bonfire at the beach after dinner."

Sam picked up Rachel and Alyssa at their houses and then we headed to the party.

Jordan's house was in the expensive part of town and had a killer ocean view. Her dad owned a chain of very successful flower shops.

I'd been to her house a couple of times, a modern-looking dwelling clinging to the side of a cliff. Jordan ran out to meet us as we pulled up.

"Everyone else is already here," she said. "C'mon, we've been waiting for you guys, to start the movie. Just leave your stuff in the hallway for now."

She led us to a theater room with heavy red velvet drapes, rows of huge leather seats, and a projector screen. There was even an antique ticket booth in one corner. If I closed my eyes just a little, I could swear I was in a real movie theater.

There were a couple of girls there who I didn't know that well. They were probably replacements for last year's graduating seniors. I'd become friends with some of the girls during my brief stint on the squad — which had been strictly to solve a mystery, of course. Someone from the team was missing.

"Where's Penny?" I asked.

Jordan avoided my eyes. "She couldn't make it," she said.

Penny? Miss an opportunity to hang with the elite crowd? I didn't think so. Besides, she was a cheerleader, even though she was an alternate. There was no way they wouldn't invite her.

I looked at Sam. "*Why* couldn't she make it?"

"It's no big deal," she replied.

"She didn't come because of me?" Penny was madder than I thought.

"Not exactly," Jordan said. "She's been saying a few things lately, and I told her that if she couldn't keep it civil, she wasn't welcome."

Sam jumped up. "Let's start the movie," she said. She turned out the lights, a clear signal that she didn't want me to ask any more questions.

After the movie, we put on our jackets and went out onto the back deck. The water looked cold and dark. Jordan passed out flashlights.

"Don't forget the s'mores," Sam said. I went back to the front hall and grabbed the grocery bag. We cut through the backyard and down a set of wooden stairs to the beach.

Jordan's parents were sitting in front of a roaring bonfire, holding hands. There were several beach chairs and a couple of blankets nearby.

When they saw us, they stood and stretched. "Time for us to head to bed," Mr. Kelley said.

"You don't have to leave," Jordan said. "Daisy's making s'mores."

Her dad gave her braid an affectionate tug. "As much as I love s'mores, we'll leave you girls to it. But not too late, okay? And make sure you put the fire out before you go to bed."

"You mean *if* they go to bed," Mrs. Kelley said wryly.

Jordan nodded and we all watched as they walked back to the house, holding hands.

Alyssa sighed. "Your parents are so romantic."

"I know," Jordan said. "Gross, isn't it?"

We all laughed, because we could tell she was proud of them.

I unpacked the ingredients. "Should I make regular s'mores or ones with white chocolate?" I asked.

"Both," they chorused.

So I did. Sam helped me pass out the snacks and we sat down to enjoy the fire, the company, and the sound of the waves crashing ashore.

"So, Daisy," Rachel said, her mouth full of chocolate. "What exactly did you do to Penny to make her so mad?"

"Nothing," I said. "Well, I accidentally spilled something on her, but I didn't think that was *that* big of a deal."

"Except you did it in front of Tyler," Alyssa said.

"So?" I was completely lost.

"So Penny has a mad crush on him," she explained.

"That's what this is all about?" I said. "Unbelievable."

"She'll get over it," Samantha said soothingly. "But maybe you should avoid her for a few days."

"I will," I said. "But what's the big deal? I mean, he's just a guy."

"Not to Penny, he's not," Jordan said.

I changed the subject. "Who's up for more s'mores?"

After we'd all drifted into a contented food coma, I collapsed into one of the beach chairs and stared out at the ocean. The moon was hiding behind a cloud, but I thought I heard a woman singing a haunting lullaby. I looked around. Nobody else seemed to have heard it, but then the sound came again, above the crash of the waves.

"Anyone want to go for a walk?" I said. Secretly, I hoped that no one, or at least no one besides Sam, would take me up on my offer. It was a private beach, so I'd be safe enough.

To my surprise, Jordan said, "I'll go with you."

"S-sure," I said. I was a little taken aback. Jordan and I got along all right, but she was more of Sam's friend than mine.

We walked along in silence for a few minutes, but then Jordan said something unexpected. "You know, my mom told me sailors used to be lured to their deaths by the sound of a mermaid singing."

"You heard it, too?" I asked.

She nodded. "I've heard singing a couple of times before, but when I went looking I never saw anything."

We fell quiet again, but this time the silence was more comfortable. The lullaby had ended, it seemed.

"It's gone," Jordan said.

But then the song started again, closer this time.

"I think it's coming from over there," I said, pointing to an outcropping of rocks near the far shore. I clicked off my flashlight. "No sense in announcing our presence."

The crescent moon peeked out from behind a cloud. We moved quietly, getting so close that we could clearly hear the words "Go down, oh, you blood-red roses."

We crept closer. There was a flash of long red hair, gleaming white skin, and a tail as someone (or something) dove off the rocks. There was a splash and a flip of a tail, and the woman disappeared into the water. Jordan and I stared at each other in amazement.

"Did you see what I saw?" I finally said.

She nodded. "I guess it's not that surprising, not in Nightshade, anyway. I've seen a lot of strange things, but I've never seen a mermaid."

I hadn't thought Jordan had noticed all the strange things that went on around her, but I had been wrong.

We headed back to the bonfire, which had died down to a faint glow.

"Hey," Sam said. "Did you guys have a good walk?"

Jordan and I exchanged smiles. "It was definitely interesting," she said.

"We were talking about going swimming, but decided we were too full," Alyssa said.

"The water is probably freezing," Jordan replied. "Let's head back to the house."

She threw sand over the coals and then grabbed a nearby sand pail and filled it with ocean water and dumped it over the fire for good measure.

I thought it might be a bit of a squeeze to have all twelve of us in Jordan's room, but there was more than enough room for all of us to spread out our sleeping bags.

We changed into our pajamas and settled in.

Jordan ignored her bed and instead put a sleeping bag next to mine and Sam's. Sam fished a bunch of fashion magazines out of her bag.

"This is the La Contessa I sold to Circe Silvertongue the other day," she said. She pointed to a large purple leather tote plastered with orange cursive LCs, for La Contessa, I assumed.

"It's . . . nice," I said lamely. Personally, I thought it was hideous, but I wasn't the one who had to carry it around.

"I saw Ms. Tray with one just like that," Rachel said idly.

"That's impossible," Samantha said.

"Why?"

"It's a one-of-a-kind item," Sam said. "See, it even says so right here. Besides, it was really expensive. More than a guidance counselor could afford."

"Maybe it's a knockoff," Jordan suggested.

"Maybe," Sam said, but she didn't sound convinced.

"What are you going to wear to the anniversary ball?" Alyssa asked, obviously bored with the subject. Talk turned to finding the perfect dress. They were still debating the merits of strapless versus halter when I fell asleep.

CHAPTER EIGHT

On Monday, at school, I felt like someone had painted a bull's-eye on my back. The air fairly reeked of suspicion, innuendo, and rumors. More than the normal high school, that is.

When I walked down the hall, the whispers started. I hadn't a clue what they were whispering about, but it couldn't be good.

In English class, I was staring at the blackboard, not really comprehending the chalk letters written there, when a voice interrupted my train of thought.

"Hey, hey, Daisy," Austin Waterman said in a whisper. I tried to ignore him. He was the biggest wannabe lady's man at Nightshade and he gave me the skeevs.

I ignored him, but looked pointedly at Ms. Tripplehorn, who was not one of the teachers who usually put up with chatter in her classroom.

"Daisy, so you and Sean, huh?"

"What are you talking about?"

He gave me a wink. "Riiight," he said, stretching the word out meaningfully.

But I wasn't catching his meaning.

Austin leaned in and said, "If you ever want to get together . . ." He put a hand on my arm. *Eeew!* I pushed him away.

"I *have* a boyfriend," I said. "And even if I didn't, I'm not interested in hooking up with you."

"Walsh is good enough for you, but I'm not?" He sneered.

"Sean is Samantha's boyfriend," I said. "He and I are just friends."

"That's not what I heard," he said.

"Where, exactly, did you hear that?"

"You're famous," he said. "Or should I say, infamous?"

I took a deep breath. He was lucky that I had my powers under control or he might have ended up toasted like a marshmallow.

"Tell me who you heard this garbage from," I said.

"I didn't hear it," he said. "I read it."

I didn't know you could read. I bit back the totally junior high comment before it escaped my lips. Antagonizing him wouldn't get me the information I needed.

He wouldn't give me the information, though, so I had to try to get it out of that pin-size brain of his.

It was like wading in gelatin, but I finally found the information I was looking for. The bathroom wall? How . . . stereotypical.

I decided to check it out for myself. Sure enough, the once pristine wall in the third-floor girls' bathroom was covered with ugliness. Who would write such horrible things?

I asked Ryan about it at lunch that day.

"There are some pretty horrid things written on the walls of the girls' bathroom," I said. "I was wondering if the boys' had been hit, too."

Ryan nodded. "It's hard not to notice," he said. "And it seems to be getting worse."

"Do you recognize the writing?" I asked.

"No," he said. "But is it just me, or does it seem like it changes all the time?"

"You mean someone writes new stuff?"

"That, too," he said. "But I meant that the writing itself changes. I was reading something when the handwriting switched from printing to cursive."

"That's . . . freaky," I replied.

"Yeah, that's what I thought," he said.

"I'm going to talk to Principal Amador about it," I said.

Ryan offered to come with me.

The principal had Ms. Tray sit in on our meeting.

"That's just awful, Daisy," she drawled when I told her the kinds of things that had been written about me. "If you ever need to talk about it, I'm here for you." Something about the way she said it seemed totally insincere.

Principal Amador promised to have the bathrooms

repainted that very day, and I thought the problem was solved. But the angry writing reappeared later that week.

"That's it," I said to Ryan after school on Wednesday. "I'm going to find out who's doing it."

"Do you need some help?"

"Not unless you want to stake out the bathroom with me," I said.

"Spending time with you? What's not to like about that scenario?" Ryan said. "Name the time."

We hung around after school until it looked like everyone had left. I half expected someone to bust us, but we didn't encounter anyone on our way to the third-floor bathroom.

I kept a sharp eye out for Ms. Tray. Her office was on the third floor, near the bathroom. Ryan might like her, but she gave me the creeps.

The bathroom was empty and the walls were pristine.

"Principal Amador must have ordered it to be painted over again," I said, but I wasn't sure how that was possible. I was sure I'd just seen new writing in there that very morning.

"Now what?" Ryan said.

"I'm sure the culprit will come back," I said. "So now we wait."

"In the girls' bathroom?" he said. He didn't try to keep the horror from his voice. "What if we get caught?"

"If you hear someone coming, just give me a kiss," I suggested.

Ryan grinned. "Will do."

A minute later, he said, "Did you hear that?"

"What?"

"Someone's coming," he said, and then swept me into his arms.

"I can't believe I fell for that," I said, several minutes later.

"It seemed like a good way to pass the time," Ryan said.

We waited there for over an hour, but no one entered the room.

I went to the sink to splash some cold water on my face. When I looked up, letters began to materialize on the wall nearest the sink. As I watched, the letters became an entire sentence, written in an angry black scrawl. "A certain Were cub in San Carlos has Ryan Mendez's green eyes."

Rage swept over me. The mirror above the sink shattered. A shard barely missed Ryan's head, but he didn't seem to care.

"What is it? What's wrong?" he said.

I pointed with a shaking hand to the writing on the wall.

"Unbelievable," Ryan said.

"Let's get out of here," I said.

"Daisy, I —"

I interrupted him. "Whoever is doing this obviously knows we're here. Let's go."

We didn't say anything until we were out of the building and in Ryan's car.

"You don't believe it, do you?" Ryan asked. His hands were clenched tightly at his side.

"Of course I do," I said.

"What?"

I finally registered the misery on my boyfriend's face. "No, I didn't mean it like that," I responded. "I meant that I know you have a little cousin in San Carlos. I met him, remember? He has green eyes, just like you."

"You scared me," Ryan said. "Was the mirror . . ."

"Me," I admitted. "I lost my temper."

He gave me a hug. "Your powers are getting stronger."

"Don't you know by now that I wouldn't believe any rumors about you. But I wonder who else knows about your cousin Ben?"

"It's not exactly a secret," Ryan said.

"True," I said. "But why would someone go to the trouble of putting it up on the bathroom wall?"

"And the bigger question is how did he or she manage to do it when we were standing right there?"

"It seems suspiciously supernatural," I replied. "I think it's time to get my sisters involved in this."

"We'll figure it out," Ryan said. "We always do."

I certainly hoped so. I wasn't sure my reputation could take much more of it.

CHAPTER NINE

When I got home, I filled my sisters in on the situation at school.

"Is it only the girls' bathroom?" Poppy asked.

"Boys' and girls'," I said. "Those third-floor bathrooms are enchanted or something. Nobody was in there besides us."

Rose looked at me shrewdly. "You're sure you weren't distracted? Even for a minute?"

My blush gave me away, but Rose's only comment was "Hmm."

"We need to have another stakeout," Poppy said.

"Maybe Natalie can help," I suggested. Natalie was Slim's girlfriend and a witch. The good kind.

"She should be able to tell us if someone has used magic," Rose said.

"I wonder if a witch can recognize another witch's style," Poppy said.

"Let's stop over at the pumpkin patch and talk to her."

Natalie lived with Slim, but she was running a pumpkin

patch on her grandmother's property, right in our neighborhood. Mrs. Mason, Natalie's grandmother, had died recently. Everyone had thought of Mrs. Mason as a kindly witch who wore pink track suits and loved gardening, but it turned out she had been helping the Scourge, creating doppelgangers. Her greenhouse had been destroyed in a terrible accident, but the former grounds were still enchanted, making for some huge pumpkins.

Natalie seemed really happy to see us, and she invited us into the small shed where she oversaw the pumpkin patch. "I'm just closing up for the day," she informed us.

"How's business?" Rose asked.

"Great," Natalie said. "The anniversary festivities have really brought a lot of people to town. I'm just hoping all the extra business helps Slim get back on his feet."

"Me, too," I said.

"These really are some superb pumpkins you have here," Poppy said as she admired a massive orange specimen in the corner of the shed. Natalie's familiar, a cat, came up and rubbed its face on the hem of Natalie's overalls and purred appreciatively.

"You can't get a better pumpkin anywhere," Natalie said. She added wistfully, "Grandma wasn't perfect, but she really did have a knack for gardening."

She offered us some hot chocolate from a thermos and we discussed our problem.

"When did you notice the writing?" Natalie asked.

"Just a few days ago," I said.

"Anything else weird going on?" she asked.

"You mean weirder than usual?" I replied. "Gossip, a bathroom wall that spews lies, and a mysterious blackmailer. Business as usual at Nightshade High."

"Hmm," Natalie said. "And you say that the writing just appeared?"

"I'm pretty sure," I said.

"Is something like that even possible?" Poppy asked.

Natalie nodded. "I know of a few spells. Or it could be a poltergeist."

Poppy went still.

"A poltergeist?" Rose repeated. She gave Poppy a worried look.

"A haunting," Natalie clarified.

"You mean a ghost?" Poppy said. At my concerned look, she added, "Don't worry. I know it's not Gage." Her chin trembled a little. "He's gone for good. I accept it."

"Can you get me in there tomorrow after school?" Natalie asked.

"Sure," I said. "The cheerleaders will be practicing, so Sam can let us in."

"I'll come, too," Poppy said.

"Should we bring anything?" Rose asked.

"You're coming, too?" I said.

"I wouldn't miss it for anything," she replied. "Besides, there's strength in numbers."

Samantha was in the gym with the other cheerleaders when my sisters got to the school.

Natalie was already there, watching their workout from the bleachers. "I always wanted to try out for cheerleading," she admitted.

"Why didn't you?" Rose asked.

"My gr-grandmother wouldn't let me," she said.

Sam said something to the other cheerleaders and then joined us.

"You guys ready?" she asked.

Natalie nodded and Sam led our little expedition through the school.

There wasn't a sign of any problem in the boys' bathroom on the third floor, but Poppy offered to keep watch.

"Are you sure you'll be okay in here alone?" I asked.

"Oh yeah," she assured us. "Maybe I'll even meet a new guy."

Sam looked scandalized. "I'm kidding," Poppy laughed. "Nobody is in the building except the cheerleaders. I've got a book and my phone, and you guys are right next door. I'll be fine." With that, the door of the boys' room swung shut behind her.

In the girls' bathroom, we found a whole wall of new graffiti. I was the featured player in most of it. While we watched, a new slur appeared on the wall. It read "Daisy Giordano: Psychic or Psycho?"

Natalie studied it for a minute. "Definitely witchcraft," she said. "But I'm not sure who. The spell itself is master level, but the workmanship is uncertain, shaky, which would indicate a new witch. Someone found an ancient spellbook is my guess."

"How many witches are there in Nightshade?" Samantha asked.

Natalie shrugged. "I have no idea," she said. "Not everyone is out, and Grandma never took me to any local coven meetings, anyway. I don't think she was happy that there was another witch in the family."

"What can we do?" I asked her.

"I think I can break the spell," she said. "I have some ingredients with me, but I'm going to have to go to the science lab to put them together."

"I'll show you where it is," Sam said. "And then I've got to get back to the squad."

"We'll wait here," I said, speaking for my sister, too. There was no way I was staying there by myself.

After they left, Rose's cell went off. She looked at the number. "I have to take this," she said. "I'll be right back. The acoustics are horrible in here."

"Wait," I said. But she was already gone. I didn't want to admit that the changing handwriting gave me serious heebie-jeebies, so I hopped up on the counter and waited for someone to come back.

It seemed like they were gone a long time, so when the door opened, I didn't even look to see who was standing there.

"It's about time," I said.

"Are you talking to yourself?" Penny asked. "Geez, Giordano, you're really losing it lately."

She had a point, but I wasn't going to let her know that.

"I thought you were my sister," I said. "What are you doing here?"

"The usual," Penny said dryly. "Not that it's any of your business."

"Why didn't you use the bathroom by the gym?" I said suspiciously.

Penny sighed, clearly annoyed. "If you must know, the downstairs bathrooms are being cleaned."

"Oh," I said. Then I noticed she was carrying a purple and orange La Contessa bag. Just like the one Sam said she'd sold to Circe. A one-of-a-kind item that suddenly seemed to be popping up everywhere. "Where did you get that bag?"

"This bag?" Penny smiled triumphantly. "You'd never be able to afford one of these in a million years," she said.

I refrained from pointing out that I'd never *want* a bag like that in a million years.

Rose walked back into the restroom. "Sorry that took so long," she said. "Oh. Hi, Penny."

Penny nodded coldly and then left.

"Any sign of the perp?" Rose asked.

I stared after Penny, lost in thought. "Maybe," I said.

Natalie came back and put the whammy on the nasty little bathroom-wall spell. I watched her as she mixed up ingredients and then sprinkled the powdered substance around the room.

"It smells like peppermint," I said.

She nodded. "I mixed peppermint, wintergreen, and chamomile into arrowroot powder."

The words disappeared, and this time, they didn't come back.

"I'm so relieved," I said. "Thanks so much, Natalie."

"Any time," she said. "But, Daisy, be careful. Someone doesn't like you very much."

"What do you mean?"

"The spell wasn't just to create random gossip. Your name was embedded in that spell," she explained. "Which means those nasty words were definitely aimed at you specifically."

"Who did you tick off this time?" Rose asked.

I sighed. "There's a long list," I said. And now Penny was at the top of it.

CHAPTER TEN

My "cooking lesson" that Saturday turned out to be a total disaster. My orders were to report to the Nightshade Harbor to help Circe cater the high school's big fundraising event on a yacht. The name on the side was *Sea Nymph*.

Practically everyone in town was going to be there, including my parents.

As instructed, I wore plain black pants with a white button-down shirt. Circe provided the aprons. Wilder's Restaurant was the official caterer, but I noticed that the aprons read "Cooking with Circe."

Most of the food had been prepped already, but there was a full, although small, kitchen on the yacht. I had assumed I'd get the chance to observe Circe in action. Instead, I ended up as a buffet runner, which meant I refilled the food on the buffet line when it was empty. And I didn't even get a fun station, like the carved prime rib station or the dessert station. Instead, I got stuck with making sure the breadbaskets were well stocked.

The room looked lovely, with white linen tablecloths and dark purple napkins.

The double doors were thrown open wide and the room was filled with people. Ms. Tray sat at a table in the front, near the bandstand. There was a clipboard in front of her. She wore a long white angora sweater dress, which made her look like a fluffy little kitten. Gold heart earrings dangled from her ears.

My parents arrived with Rose and Nicholas. Since the breadbaskets were secure, I went to say hi. But Ms. Tray beat me to it.

"Mr. and Mrs. Giordano, so nice to see you," she said. She greeted them like they were long lost friends. For a minute, I thought she was going to try to hug my father. But at the last minute, she changed her mind and offered him her hand.

Dad took it and shook it vigorously. The warmth of his smile made Ms. Tray flutter her eyelashes girlishly.

"Who is this gorgeous girl?" she asked, obviously talking about Rose.

"This is Rose. She's my oldest and is a sophomore at UC Nightshade," Dad said proudly.

"Well, bless your heart," Ms. Tray said. "Aren't you just the cutest little thing?"

Rose said all the polite things and then excused herself to go talk to Mr. Todeschi, her old band teacher.

As Ms. Tray continued chatting animatedly with my father, my mother whispered into my ear, "Who is that woman?"

"She's the new guidance counselor at school," I said.

"She's about as subtle as a barracuda," Mom said. "Oh, there's Chief Mendez and Ryan. Keep your father company while I go say hi."

But I had to get back to the buffet table. I was reluctant to leave my dad alone with Ms. Tray, but he assured me that he would be fine.

Stuck behind the buffet table, I kept my eyes glued to the guidance counselor and my dad. Their conversation looked so innocuous, but I still kept watching. My father was talking and laughing. I used every ounce of my powers to listen in.

At first, I couldn't tune in properly, since there were so many other conversations going on in the room, and I think some dolphins around the boat might have been interfering, too. But I finally managed to tune out everyone else and hone in on the two of them.

Ms. Bea Tray spoke with a honey-laced southern accent and had soft blond hair and big blue eyes. But she was pure poison. A trace of venom threaded through her words.

"Your daughter," she said. "Bless her heart, but she is not living up to her potential."

"She's not?" My dad's smile turned to a frown.

"If only Daisy would concentrate on her studies, instead of . . ." Ms. Tray paused delicately. Probably deciding where to stick the knife.

"Instead of what?" My dad sounded almost panic-stricken. I wondered what lies she'd make up this time.

"I don't want to be indelicate."

"Please, tell me if there is something wrong with my daughter," he replied.

"I've heard something quite disturbing about her, it's true," she said.

Disturbing? Between school, work, cooking lessons, volunteering, and trying to spend time with Ryan and my family, I didn't have any time for anything *disturbing*, even if I'd wanted to.

Ms. Tray was trying to cause trouble, I was sure of it. I clenched my hands into fists and the plastic serving tongs I held snapped in two.

"Something wrong?" Sam said, puzzled. She and Sean stood on the other side of the buffet, plates piled high with food.

I put a finger to my lips. "Hang on a second," I said.

But I'd lost the connection.

What else was Ms. Tray telling my father? She was playing Dad like a country fiddle, exploiting his paranoia.

"Hey, what do you know about the guidance counselor?" I asked Samantha.

"Not much," she said. She gave me a searching look.

"She said that I better pray for a football scholarship," said

Sean. "Come on, babe, let's eat," he said to Samantha. "I want to come back for seconds."

My friends went to find a table, and I looked back over at Ms. Tray and my dad. She put her hand on his arm and leaned in close, like she was telling him a secret. That's when I noticed Penny Edwards, lingering near my father and Ms. Tray, doing the old-fashioned kind of eavesdropping. She gave me a wicked smile that made me want to throw her off the boat. Clearly, she had overheard whatever I had missed.

Ryan and his dad headed my way.

"Hi, Chief Mendez," I said. I leaned across the buffet and wrapped an arm around Ryan. "I didn't know you were going to be here tonight."

He gave his dad a little sock on the arm. "Dad needed a date."

Chief Mendez chuckled and then said, "It's quite the shindig. I've never seen your mom so dressed up."

Mom was on her way back to Dad. Excellent news. Mom would be able to extricate him from Ms. Tray's clutches.

"Let's dance," Ryan suggested.

"I can't," I said. "I'm working."

I glanced over at Ms. Tray. She was still yakking away, but Mom had arrived to save the day.

"Come on," Ryan urged, "Let's check out the view from the deck."

"Okay, but just for a few minutes," I said, and popped out from behind the buffet.

When we got up to the deck, it was empty.

I told Ryan about what I had seen and heard. "That's all I need," I said. "For my dad to be more paranoid."

"Maybe it's not as bad as you think," he said. I knew he was trying to comfort me, but it wasn't working. I had a bad feeling in the pit of my stomach.

"We should go back," I said. But I didn't really want to.

Ryan put his hands on my waist. "We should stay," he said. He bent his head and gave me a tiny kiss.

"But what about the fundraiser? My dad?"

"Just five minutes."

Several very enjoyable minutes later, I stopped kissing him.

"Ryan, we've been gone for ages. Circe is going to kill me."

We practically ran back. Nobody seemed to notice that we'd been gone. At least that's what I thought until Circe caught up with me.

"Daisy, where have you been? I've been looking for you everywhere."

"Sorry, I went out for a breath of air and just lost track of time," I said.

For a minute, I thought she was going to explode, but instead she smiled. "I was young and in love once," she said. She sighed and her eyes grew distant, changing from an icy green to a soft blue. She shook herself and the ice returned. "Don't let it happen again. Now go fill the breadbaskets."

A little while later, I spotted someone I needed to talk to. I'd tried to corner Wolfgang Paxton several times at school, but he always managed to avoid me. Now he was stuck on a boat in the middle of the harbor, however. He couldn't avoid me here.

I found him refilling his plate at the roast beef station. "I said rare," he snapped at the server.

"Hi, there, Wolfie," I said.

"What do you want?" he asked.

"That's not very nice," I replied. "A little birdy told me that you might need help."

"I don't," he said, but he still refused to face me.

"You do," I said. "Someone is blackmailing you. Maybe I can help."

"Like you helped me last time?" he said scornfully. "Thanks, but no thanks."

"You'd rather just give in to their demands?" I said.

"I can handle it," he said. "It's not that much money." He realized he'd slipped up and inadvertently admitted he was being blackmailed. He swore under his breath and stalked off.

I felt Circe's eyes on me and hurried back to my breadbaskets. Hardly the learning experience I'd dreamed of when I'd first won the lessons.

A little later, I noticed Lilah Porter and her family sitting at one of the tables. I waved to her, but she didn't look like she was having much fun. Her hair was soaking wet. Her father looked over at her and frowned.

After the party ended and the yacht docked, Circe had me scrubbing pots and pans until midnight.

When I got home, Mom was in bed, but Dad was waiting up and he didn't look happy.

"Hi, Dad," I said. "Did you have a nice chat with Ms. Tray?"

"It was . . . illuminating," he said. "I'm very concerned about your relationship with that boy," Dad said. "I've heard things."

"What kind of things?"

"It doesn't matter," my dad said. "I don't see a future between the two of you."

"So you're psychic now?" I said. "It's my senior year. Do I really have to decide every bit of my future right now?"

"Don't you think you should be thinking about the future of your relationship? Can you trust him if you both go to different colleges?"

"Don't you think you should give Ryan the benefit of the doubt? Maybe a chance to defend himself? How can he do that if you won't even tell me what you heard?"

"I heard that he's dangerous," my father replied.

"Dangerous?" I snorted. "Ryan? You mean because he's a werewolf?"

"That's not what I mean at all," he replied. "I've never cared about that sort of thing. You know that."

"Then what's the problem?"

"I don't think he's a good influence on you."

The conversation was going nowhere. "Look, Dad, I'm not going to break up with Ryan."

"You'll do what you're told," he said sternly. "I am your father."

"My father, who has been gone for the last six years," I said. "You can't expect to come home and find everything the same as when you left."

"I don't," he said. "But I do expect you to listen to me."

"Listening isn't agreeing," I replied.

"Promise me you'll think about it," he said. "That's all I ask."

"I promise, if you'll promise to give Ryan a chance."

But he wouldn't even consider it. He squared his shoulders. "You are grounded," he said.

"What? That's not fair," I said. The plates in the cupboard rattled and I forced myself to calm down.

"You are not allowed to go out with that boy until further notice," he said, his voice rising.

Poppy poked her head into the kitchen. "What's all the shouting about?" she said, looking from Dad to me in bewilderment.

"He's trying to ruin my life, that's all," I said.

I ran from the room before I started to cry. I stomped up the stairs and into my bedroom, slamming the door behind me.

What had gotten into my father? How was I going to con-vince him that Ryan could be trusted? Or more important, that *I* could be trusted?

CHAPTER ELEVEN

Getting to see Ryan again was the only good part of going back to school on Monday.

I vented to Sam about my problem. She was an expert on relationships. Practically every guy in school wanted to date her, but she and Sean were as steady as ever.

"What should I do?" I asked her. We were in the library during study hall.

Sam pushed her history book in front of me when the librarian looked over at us.

"My father is completely unreasonable about Ryan," I said, ignoring both the librarian's glare and the history book.

"Do you think it's because of, you know, the *grrr* thing?" Sam said.

"You mean because Ryan's" — I lowered my voice — "a werewolf? Of course not."

Dad had adjustments to deal with, but I knew it wouldn't bother him that two of his daughters were dating werewolves. Or that his other daughter was pining over a ghost.

"Maybe he's trying to make up for lost time," Sam suggested.

"But there's no way he can really do that," I pointed out. "I'm not a little kid anymore, no matter how much he wishes I were."

"I don't know, Daisy," Sam admitted. "I figured he would loosen up as time went on, but that doesn't seem to be the case."

"No kidding," I said. "Ever since he talked to that guidance counselor —"

"*Mis*guidance counselor is more like it," Sam said. "She must have told him something pretty bad."

Suddenly I spotted Penny, lurking in the stacks nearby. If anyone knew what Ms. Tray said, it was her.

I followed Penny down a deserted aisle. "Tell me what Ms. Tray said to my father at the fundraiser," I demanded.

"Your father?"

"Don't play stupid, Penny. I saw you listening in on their conversation."

"So?"

"So, what were they talking about?"

"What is your problem, Giordano?" she said.

"What's *your* problem?" I could feel the tension ratchet up a notch, but I couldn't help myself. The beads on the necklace she was wearing cascaded to the floor.

"That was my favorite necklace," she said.

"What were they talking about?" I demanded again.

"Nothing," she said as she picked beads up off the tile.

I didn't believe her.

"That was a pretty long conversation about nothing," I said.

Penny just glared at me. "The world doesn't revolve around you, you know. You think everyone is talking about you? Just wait until you find out what it's really like to have everyone whispering."

"Is that a threat?"

"It's a promise," she said, before stomping off.

"Real original, Penny," I hissed.

But Penny topped me. "Just you wait, Daisy. Just you wait."

The librarian approached, clearly miffed about the noise Penny and I were making. I think she was about to write me up, but luckily the bell rang at that very second.

I was grateful to have a shift at Slim's that Friday. Work was the only thing that got me out of the house since being grounded.

I missed the home football game but was regaled with my boyfriend's football prowess during the minor rush after the game. I didn't get to hear it from Ryan, because he was out celebrating with the rest of the team.

Finally, the hungry fans and tired tourists were all fed and Slim's gradually emptied out. My feet were grateful that it was almost closing time.

Flo approached me. "Just so you know," she said conspiratorily. "The city council is handling that blackmail thing."

"Really?" I said. "Who do they think is sending the notes?"

"No clue yet," Flo said. "But if you know anyone who gets one, make sure they report it to the council."

I wondered if Wolfie had brought his note to the council's attention.

After a long pause, Flo said, "Daisy, I hate to ask, but would you mind if I left the lockup to you? I . . . I have something to do."

She glanced over at a two-top, where the drummer for Side Effects May Vary sat, using two straws to drum on the table. When he saw us staring at him, he gave Flo a slow smile and a wave.

Flo had a date! I grinned at her. "You go ahead. Vinnie's waiting."

Flo had thrown a button-down sweater over her work tee but managed to make the outfit look like she'd spent hours getting ready.

"Have fun, but don't stay out too late. You have to work in the morning, too," I called after her.

She turned and said, "Don't push it."

After they left, I decided to consult with Lil again and see if she could give me a hint about the blackmail notes. "A little help, please," I said, as I dropped a bunch of quarters into the slot.

Lil played immediately, which I took as a good sign, but I wasn't sure what her song choice meant. The song she chose was "Pig" by Weezer. Did that mean the blackmailer was a pig? Circe had a pet pig. It was a start.

I got another clue when she played a second song. "My Body Is a Cage" by Arcade Fire. But I still didn't know what they meant.

By the time I'd done all the closing chores and locked up for the night, it was late and Main Street was deserted. Fog had rolled in from the ocean and covered everything in a fine gray mist. I was glad that I had the car for a change, even though I'd had to park it around the corner.

I wasn't thinking about much of anything except getting home to bed, so I didn't really pay attention when I heard footsteps behind me. Probably a tourist straggler.

But some little voice inside my head told me to stop, to see what the person (at least I hoped it was a person) behind me would do. I fumbled in my bag and pretended to look for my keys, which were already clenched in my right hand.

The footsteps stopped, too. I felt warning prickles at the back of my neck. Someone was watching me. Following me. My heart rate accelerated, but I took a deep breath and tried to remain calm.

I suppressed the urge to run and walked slowly to my car. I sent out a little psychic probe to see if anyone was there but came up against a mental block of some kind. Whoever was behind me knew me or at least knew of my abilities. Knew enough about me, anyhow, to block my telekinesis.

I was almost at my car. "I know you're there," I said in as loud a voice as I could muster, but it came out a scared little squeak. I told myself it was probably someone harmless, just somebody trying to scare me. Someone like Penny.

"Penny, I know you're there," I said, louder this time. I was proud of the way my voice hardly trembled at all.

There was a blast of frigid air, so cold that I started to shiver.

Then nothing. I held my breath until I heard the sound of footsteps receding. I hurried to my car and got in, clicking the door locks as quickly as I could before I put the car into gear and went home.

Rose was still out, but Poppy was in her room, studying.

"Do you feel like taking a break? I'll make you a snack."

Poppy looked up from her textbook. "You look like death warmed over," she said. "I'll take a break and you can tell me all about it."

We went down to the kitchen and while I made hot chocolate, I told her what happened.

She looked at me doubtfully. "Are you sure it wasn't just your imagination working overtime?"

"No, it wasn't my imagination," I said. "Someone was following me, I'm sure of it."

I put the chocolate in front of her. "Do you want marshmallows?"

She made a face.

I shrugged. "More for me, then."

We talked about the possibilities. Poppy was less positive than I was that it was Penny.

"I know she's mad at you," she said. "But I can't see her stalking you."

"I can," I replied. I went to bed without convincing Poppy I was right.

CHAPTER TWELVE

My dad drove me to my cooking lesson with Circe that Saturday. We'd bought another car when Dad came home, and Mom had optimistically hoped that he'd jump right back into academia. That hadn't happened. He still hadn't heard back from the interview he had a couple of weeks before, and he didn't seem to have any other options on the horizon. Meanwhile, the car gathered dust, for the most part, but we weren't allowed to take it, because Mom wanted to have it available for Dad to use.

"You've been looking a little tired lately," he remarked on the drive over to Wilder's.

"Being a chef isn't as easy as I thought it would be," I admitted.

"Are you rethinking a culinary career?" he asked.

"No," I said. "I really like it. It's just working at Slim's, cooking lessons, school . . ." I didn't mention my boyfriend, since we were still at odds over my relationship with Ryan.

"Daisy, can I ask you a question?"

Uh-oh, I thought. *Here it comes.*

"Why did you give up gymnastics? You were quite serious about it."

Dad was bringing up a sore subject.

"I didn't give up gymnastics, Dad. It gave me up."

"What do you mean?"

"Haven't you noticed? I grew about eight inches since you were gone. I'm too tall for gymnastics now."

Dad was a little shaky behind the wheel, but he delivered me in one piece and said, "Call me when you're finished tonight and I'll come by and pick you up."

"Will do," I said. "I shouldn't be too late."

Circe looked like a wreck when I got there. There was flour in her hair and her normally immaculate coif was in disarray.

"Daisy, get your apron on and get the vegetables chopped."

Hello to you, I thought. I threw on an apron and washed my hands and then got started on an enormous pile of veggies. I have to admit I cheated a little when no one was looking. A lot of people knew of my psychic abilities, but I didn't want anyone to think I was showing off.

The kitchen reeked of tension and sweat. "What's going on?" I asked Sabrina, one of the wait staff.

"We're double-booked and the sous-chef didn't show up for work tonight," she replied. "Gotta go. I'm slammed out there."

It wasn't just Circe who was suffering. The entire staff of

Wilder's, with the possible exception of Bianca, was scared of Circe when she was in a *good* mood. She was terrifying when she was in a bad mood. The dishwasher dropped a plate and the whole place sucked in its collective breath when Circe's head whipped around, quick as a snake.

Her eyes gleamed green fire, a sure sign that an explosion was imminent. Instead, she only barked, "I need more pork chops!"

Balthazar let out a tiny whimper when he heard that.

I tore lettuce by hand for salads (chopping it bruised the lettuce) and whipped up gallons of Circe's secret recipe salad dressing. "The salad dressing is done," I said.

"Not quite," she said, then sniffed. She rummaged in her pocketed apron and pulled out what looked like a small bag of herbs and sprinkled it into the dressing. "Now it's a Circe Silvertongue creation," she said.

For the next two hours, I sautéed, chopped, stirred, and sweated. I kept hoping the sous-chef would show up, but there was no sign of him. Several times, Balthazar trotted up and squealed. It sounded like he was trying to tell me something, but when he saw Circe glaring at him, he retreated to his little bed outside her office.

I saw Circe get something from her office and throw it into a pot. She glanced around and I quickly averted my eyes. When I looked up again, all I saw was Circe's eyes glow green and then a little puff of smoke rose from the pot. It didn't *look* like she was working on a new recipe. In fact, it looked decidedly suspicious, but I got too busy for any more snooping.

I was relieved when I had a chance to take a bathroom break. When I came out of the bathroom, Balthazar was waiting for me in the hallway. He snorted, then started trotting to the side door that led to the garden. I could tell he wanted me to follow him.

I looked back at the kitchen nervously, but Circe was so busy, she didn't even seem to realize I was gone. I decided a little break wouldn't hurt. Besides, I was supposed to be getting cooking lessons, not indentured servitude.

It was chilly in the garden. I walked quickly, following Balthazar's curly little tail in the dark. My heart started pounding harder when he entered the maze.

"No!" I yelped, and stopped in my tracks.

The pig turned around and squealed and stamped. I really did not want to go into the maze, but I had a feeling there was something in there I needed to see. I took a breath and went after Balthazar.

The pig turned a few corners, then stopped, nosing at something under the hedge. I reached down and felt something cold and metallic. It was a cooking pot. I picked it up and looked inside, to see the charred remains of something. I touched a hard red substance crusted to the inside of the pot.

"Wax," I whispered. Balthazar was snorting like crazy next to me. Suddenly I realized that this must be a blackmail letter.

Probably one that was sent to Circe. Too bad there wasn't much of it left. I picked up a charred piece of paper still partially intact. I could read the words *sorcery* and *missing*, but I had no idea what those words meant or why Circe had torched the letter. Balthazar looked up at me with pleading eyes. "I'm sorry," I said, "But there's not much here to read."

The two of us headed back to the restaurant and slipped surreptitiously inside. The rest of the evening was a blur, but eventually the rush died down. During cleanup, Bianca walked into the kitchen. "Daisy, your boyfriend is here," she said. "He's waiting on the terrace for you."

Circe snorted. "Men can't be trusted, you know. Balthazar is the only one I can rely on. He'll never leave me." She reached down to pet Balthazar, but he shied away.

Ryan was here? My dad was supposed to pick me up. I tore off my apron and went to find him.

"I'm surprised to see you here," I said. "Pleasantly surprised, of course."

He made an effort to smile. "Work and school are the only places I can see you these days," he said. "And I need to talk to you about something."

"I'll get my stuff."

As soon as we got in the car, I was about to blurt out what I had learned about Circe, but he handed me a note. I recognized that heavy white paper and red wax seal right away. "You're being blackmailed, too?"

Ryan nodded. "My dad is going to go ballistic when he sees this."

"So you haven't told him anything?"

He shook his head. "Not yet. I wanted to talk to you first. I didn't want to worry him. He's been . . . stressed lately."

"The council already knows about the blackmailer," I reminded him. "I think we should take this to them. They have to know."

"I know," he said. "But I don't want Dad to know *I* got a blackmail note."

Why would Ryan want to keep something like that from his dad? It didn't make any sense.

"But —" I said.

"I'll tell him when I'm ready, Daisy. Now, are you going to help me or not?"

I knew he was worried, but I wasn't going to let him growl at me just because he'd been the victim of a little blackmail.

"*Of course* I'll help you," I said. "But you don't need to snap at me just because I told you what I think, which is that you're making a mistake."

His face closed and I decided I better not push the issue.

There was an awkward silence. Then we both said, "I'm sorry."

"I didn't mean to growl," he said.

"And I didn't mean to lecture," I said. "Now tell me exactly where you were when you found the note."

"It was in my gym bag," Ryan said.

"Like Wolfie's," I said. "Maybe it's someone who goes to school here."

"Not necessarily," Ryan disagreed with me. "It could be a teacher, or a visitor, or even someone who isn't so easily seen."

"You can't think Slim would do something like this!" The thought that my boss could be involved just wasn't possible. He was one of the good guys. Plus, he got a letter, too.

"No," Ryan said. "Not Slim. But he's not the only . . ."

"Invisible man," I finished for him. "Yeah, I'm pretty sure he is, at least in Nightshade."

"I mean, he's not the only one we can't see."

"Right," I said. "There are ghosts and maybe vampires, if it's true they can turn into some sort of fog. And shifters."

"It could be a regular old sneaky human," Ryan said.

"Like who?" *Sneaky* reminded me of Ms. Tray, but I couldn't really picture her tiptoeing into the boys' locker room.

"One of the coaches," he suggested. "Or someone on the football team."

"I don't think so," I said. "I saw the same kind of letter at Circe's."

"Why didn't you say so before now?" Ryan cried.

"I was going to," I said. "But then you told me your news." I paused. "The weird thing is, Circe burned her letter. I wonder why she didn't turn it over to the council. They are investigating this, after all."

"I think we should talk to Mr. Bone," Ryan said.

We headed to the funeral home with the hope of catching him there.

Normally, Mr. Bone wore loud Hawaiian shirts and shorts. He loved to golf and always had a smile on his face.

We caught up with him in his office. He wore a formal black suit and tie. There was no sign of his normally cheerful demeanor.

"Is this a bad time?" I asked him. "We wanted to talk to you, if you have a minute."

Mr. Bone looked at his watch. "Unfortunately, I only have a few minutes. There was a death in San Carlos and we are handling the arrangements. One of their best high school football players died suddenly."

Ryan shook his head sadly. "I heard about that," he said. "That's why they called off the game a couple weeks back."

"If he died weeks ago, why is he just being buried now?" I asked.

"They did an autopsy first," Mr. Bone explained. I was curious to hear more details, but I knew Mr. Bone wouldn't gossip about his work.

We told him about Ryan's letter. I knew I should report what I saw at Wilder's, too. I hesitated because I didn't want to get on Circe's bad side, but I did want the blackmailer stopped.

I gulped and then blurted out, "I think I saw a note in Circe

Silvertongue's office at Wilder's. And then tonight I found the burnt remains of it in the garden maze."

Mr. Bone was smiling a *Don't you worry* smile, which made me worry.

"We'll look into the Circe situation," he said. Then, probably sensing my anxiety, he added, "We'll keep your name out of it."

That was going to be very hard to do, I was sure of it.

I had wondered why Circe would want to hide being blackmailed, but then a different angle occurred to me. Maybe those letters were written *by* Circe, not *to* her. "Do you think Circe could be the blackmailer?" I asked.

"What would make you think that?" Mr. Bone asked.

"She's a highly successful chef, with her own cookbooks, television show, everything," Ryan pointed out. "Why would she need the money?"

"Money?" I said. "Did your letter ask you for money?"

"Not yet," Ryan said. "But what else could the blackmailer want?"

"It's just that she's . . ." I paused, uncertain about how to continue.

"Difficult? Demanding?" Mr. Bone supplied. "Yes, but she is not a blackmailer."

I hated to admit it, but I was disappointed. Circe was my only suspect and I didn't have any other leads. "What makes you so sure?"

"Circe has . . . too much at stake herself," Mr. Bone explained, then quickly changed the subject by asking Ryan to show him the note he'd received.

Ryan held out the note with its hateful red seal. I would be happy if I never saw that particular red seal again.

Mr. Bone put on his reading glasses. "The handwriting is the same as the other notes," he observed.

Ryan leaned closer. "It's fancy. It looks kind of . . ." He hesitated, then threw me a look.

"Girly?" I asked. "It's okay. I noticed it, too." The calligraphy was full of flourishes. Despite its elegant look, the message was altogether menacing.

There was a tiny triple heart in the pattern of the seal. Where had I seen that particular pattern before? It bothered me the rest of the night, but I couldn't remember.

"If I hear anything else, I'll be in touch," Mr. Bone said. "Now, if you'll excuse me, I have some work to do."

It must be hard to tend to the dead, I thought. Mr. Bone always seemed so happy, but he was noticeably downcast. I couldn't blame him.

Ryan and I got back in the car. "I better get home," I said regretfully.

"Daisy, I haven't been alone with you in a week," Ryan said. "I'm dying here. And it's going to be a full moon soon."

Which meant my boyfriend would be howling at the moon for a few days.

"I miss you, too," I said softly.

"Why are your parents being so strict?" Ryan asked. "It's your senior year."

"It's just my dad. He doesn't want me seeing you for a while."

"Maybe we ought to —"

I kissed the words from his lips. "Maybe we ought to nothing," I said, after a long minute. Then I kissed him again, just to show him exactly how much I'd missed him. He had evidently been missing me, as well, because he kissed me deeply. Somehow I ended up horizontal across the front seat.

The car radio played songs about being in love, and I forgot about everything, including the time. The world receded until all I could think about was Ryan, the touch of his lips, the feel of his skin against mine.

Of course, that's what made it completely embarrassing when a squad car pulled up. And not just any police officer got out. No, it had to be the chief of police.

"Ryan, it's your dad," I whispered, frantically pushing him away.

"Quit joking," he said.

"I'm *not!*" Ryan heard the panic in my voice and sat up quickly.

"Your shirt," I whispered, as Ryan's dad approached the car. "It's unbuttoned."

Ryan fumbled with his buttons, but I thought he wasn't going to get his shirt done up in time, so I decided to help him.

I mean, my telekinesis skills were perfect in a time like this, right? Wrong.

I was so flustered that my concentration was messed up and I popped all the buttons off his shirt, sending them flying in every direction.

"Sorry," I said, but even under extreme pressure, I still had time to admire his chest.

"It's okay," he said. He grabbed a T-shirt from his gym bag and quickly switched shirts.

"Daisy, Ryan, out of the car please," Chief Mendez said.

Humiliation couldn't begin to describe what I was feeling as we scrambled out.

"We weren't doing anything wrong," I said. I could tell that Chief Mendez was unhappy, and I didn't want Ryan to get into trouble.

"I know," the chief said. "But it's very late, and nobody knew where you were. Your parents are frantic. I got a call that you were missing."

"My parents?" I said. "You mean my dad."

Chief Mendez nodded gravely.

"I'll take her home, Dad," Ryan offered, but the chief glowered at him.

"I think I'd better take care of that, son," he said sternly.

Ryan got out of his car and locked it up. "I'm coming with you," he said, placing a reassuring hand on my shoulder. "I have something to talk to my dad about, anyway."

I was glad to hear that Ryan would be coming clean about the blackmail letter to his dad. But then I suffered the humiliation of having the chief drive me home like I was some kind of juvenile delinquent.

Which, technically, I guess I was. I'd snuck out with Ryan behind my parents' backs. Not exactly the behavior of someone who was trustworthy. But I'd gotten used to coming and going as I pleased. Mom had trusted me. Why couldn't Dad?

He was waiting at the door. He shook hands with the chief and then ushered me inside. There was no sign of my mom or Rose or Poppy.

"Where is everyone else?" I asked.

"Your mother is in bed," he replied. "And your sisters are out."

I raised an eyebrow.

"Your mother doesn't know you were gone," my dad said. "I didn't want to worry her."

I didn't want to break it to him that I'd been out much later, and in far more dangerous circumstances. Somehow, I didn't think he'd take any comfort in that fact.

Instead of talking to him like a mature high school senior, I gave him the silent treatment and retreated to my bedroom. I punched my pillow as I tried to figure out how to get through to my father, but the pillow wouldn't talk and I was out of ideas.

CHAPTER **THIRTEEN**

My alarm went off way too early the next morning. I rolled over and groaned. Early shift at Slim's and I was going to be late if I didn't move it. I grabbed a quick shower and dressed in some relatively clean work clothes before I dashed out the door.

When I got there, however, it was absolute chaos, so nobody even noticed I was a little late.

Flo had her hands full of frozen steaks, and although my boss wasn't exactly visible, I could see the freezer door opening and closing. There were pools of water everywhere.

"What happened?" I said.

"Freezer died," she said. She set down the steaks. "Slim's having a fire sale."

"Huh?"

She shrugged. "We were barely keeping our heads above water before this. Commercial freezers are really expensive. Slim's ready to close."

"He can't do that!" I protested.

The freezer door slammed. "I don't have any choice, Daisy," Slim said. He didn't sound like himself.

"Slim, maybe it can be fixed —"

"Daisy, someone broke in and did this deliberately," he said.

I noticed something else. "Where's the jukebox?" I said.

"What?"

"Where is the jukebox?" I said, panicked. "You didn't sell her, did you?"

"Of course not," he replied.

Flo said, "I put Lil in the office after closing last night."

"Why would you do that?"

"After Circe Silvertongue came by the other day, I started locking Lil in the office after closing."

"A lock isn't going to stop a sorceress," Slim said.

I gaped at him. "She's a sorceress? Why didn't anyone tell me?"

"I thought you knew," he said. "I've heard people talking about her at the restaurant. She's pretty powerful. I'm not sure what we can do to stop her."

"A lock warded by a witch should do the trick," Flo said triumphantly. "I knew she was up to no good, so I had Natalie put a ward on the office."

Slim surveyed the freezer ruefully. "I wish you'd had her ward the entire place," he said.

"I will now," Flo promised.

"Do you think Circe used magic to ruin your freezer?" I asked.

"Probably," Flo said.

"Then could Natalie use magic to reverse the damage?"

Slim picked up the phone and started dialing. "Daisy, you're a genius."

An hour later, the freezer was running again and Slim had calmed down enough to decide that he wasn't going to close Slim's, at least not yet.

I wanted to blame it all on Circe, but part of me wondered if there was anyone else in town who had something against Slim.

After the freezer was up and running, Natalie warded the entire building. I watched her do it and marveled at how quickly her power had grown since she was out from under her grandmother's thumb.

Afterward, I helped Flo move the jukebox into her usual spot. Flo hadn't even plugged the machine in before Lil let forth a stream of songs.

I recognized "Blackmail" by the Runaways, "Help, I'm Alive" by Metric, and "Blackhearted Love" by PJ Harvey.

"What's wrong with her?" Flo said.

The jukebox was definitely agitated. The last song cut off and there was silence. Then she repeated the sequence one more time before finally going mum.

"She's trying to tell us something," I said. Lil had never been so talkative, but I couldn't figure out the clues she was giving me.

Flo nodded. "Do you have any idea what she's talking about?"

"Unfortunately, no," I said.

Flo shrugged and then bent down to plug in the jukebox.

"Can I borrow a quarter?" I asked.

Flo handed me a stack of shiny coins. "We need all the help we can get."

The quarters went in and I looked at my selection choices. Maybe it was time I tried speaking her language. I punched in E4, which today was "Talk to Me." Nothing. My next try was "Tell Me" by Stevie Ray Vaughan, then "Tell Me Something" by Selena Gomez.

Lil didn't respond for a long time. Finally, the music started playing. The song was "Help" by the Beatles.

This time I got the message, loud and clear.

I put my hand out and touched the warm smooth surface of the jukebox. "I'll help you, Lil," I said.

Fortunately, we had a steady stream of customers. Samantha showed up with a group of anniversary party volunteers, who grabbed a table in the corner. Nurse Phillips and the rest of her band filled up one of the booths. I headed toward the Side Effects May Vary booth, but Flo waved me off and took their order instead.

Gradually Slim's bad mood lifted. The ticket wheel shook occasionally with the force of his agitation, but by the time the breakfast rush had ended, Slim was back to his usual self.

The people at Samantha's table, however, didn't look very happy. In fact, Lilah Porter was in tears. I asked Samantha what was up, when she approached me during my break at the counter.

Samantha said, "Didn't you hear?"

"Hear what?" I said.

"Lilah Porter got one of those notes a few weeks back. And later, someone sent her parents some incriminating photos."

"Photos of what?"

"She didn't say," Sam replied. "But she's getting shipped off to boarding school."

"But it's her senior year," I said.

"Harsh, huh?" Sam said. "But her parents won't budge."

A thought occurred to me. "Is Lilah . . . you know?"

"Why don't you ask her yourself?" Sam suggested. She motioned to Lilah to join us at the counter.

Lilah's eyes were rimmed in red and she held a box of Kleenex. "What do you want?" she said. She sniffled noisily.

"Daisy has a couple of questions for you," Sam said.

I wasn't sure how to start. "So you're leaving for boarding school soon?" I finally said.

"Yeah, can you believe it?" she said bitterly. "One little slip-up and my parents couldn't wait to ship me off."

"About that slip-up," I said. "I heard you got a blackmail letter."

"I thought it was a joke or something," Lilah said. "At first."

"Then what happened?"

"Then all hell broke loose," she said. "My parents got the photos in the mail and it was all over."

"Can you show us the photos?" Sam asked.

"No," Lilah said. "My dad was so mad, he put them through the shredder."

"This is kind of a sensitive question," I said. I dropped my voice and made sure nobody else in the diner was listening in. "But do you happen to have any . . . powers?"

"You mean, am I psychic or anything?" she asked. "Like your family? Not exactly."

"But there is something different about you," I said. It was a statement, not a question. I had a pretty good idea that Lilah was like the blackmailer's other victims. She had some sort of paranormal gift, although she obviously didn't want anyone to know about it.

She nodded. "Let's just say that there's a reason I was protesting showers after PE." Lilah had successfully lobbied to make showers after gym class optional.

"You mean . . . ?"

"Mermaid," she whispered. "On my mother's side. My dad is freaked."

"There's nothing wrong with being a mermaid," I said.

"Tell that to my father," Lilah replied.

"And the photos?" Sam asked.

"Midnight swim. I thought I was alone, but obviously I wasn't."

"Do you remember when the photo was taken?"

She shrugged. "Right after school started. I wanted to get one last swim in before the water got too chilly. Even mermaids get cold."

"Did the note ask for money?" I asked her.

"Not the first one," she said.

"There was more than one?"

"Yes. Three, total," she said. "But I didn't find the last two until it was too late."

"Where did you find it?" Sam asked. I was pretty sure I already knew the answer to her question and Lilah's answer confirmed it.

"In my gym bag," she said. "But I'd lost track of it for a few days and I finally found it in lost and found. So anybody could have put the note in there."

"Do you still have the notes?"

"Nope," she said. "I gave them to my dad."

"Anything else you can tell us?"

"Just that I hope you catch whoever is doing this," she said.

"We will," I said. "E-mail me if you think of anything else." I wrote down my e-mail address and cell phone number on a piece of paper and handed it to her.

Lilah headed back to the table.

I didn't say anything until she was out of earshot. "Boarding school."

"Yeah. Boarding school. And the worst part is that they found a school miles from any ocean or river. No pool. Lilah will be miserable," Sam said.

"Did you know about her?" I asked.

"I can keep a secret," she said. "And Nightshade's full of them."

She was right. Nightshade was full of secrets, but wouldn't be for long if we didn't stop the blackmailer.

CHAPTER FOURTEEN

I wished I could do some investigating after work that day, but Dad had laid down the law. I had to come home right after school and work, no dates — not even group dates — until further notice. I'm pretty sure Mom stopped him from checking me into a convent, but just barely. She was busy with a case, which meant long hours and a certain distracted air.

"Mom, can't you talk to him? Please?" I said.

"I will, but Daisy, your father is still adjusting to being back in Nightshade," she said. "Could you please be tolerant for a little while longer?"

I sighed. "He's not like this with Rose or Poppy."

"You're still in high school, Daisy," she pointed out. "And I can't really say I disagree with your father's decision to ground you after your shenanigans last night."

"Mom, it's not my fault that Dad missed out on half of my childhood," I said.

"It's not his fault, either," she said gently. "Maybe you should try to remember that."

I nodded. "I'll try," I said. A tiny part of me *was* still angry that he'd been gone so long, but it was time to get over it. I spent the rest of the weekend looking at old photographs of Dad and me.

Monday at school, Ms. Tray called me out of class. I headed to her office begrudgingly. I'd avoided her as long as I could, but I'd run out of excuses.

I ran into Penny Edwards in the hallway. She put her nose in the air and tried to ignore me, but I stepped in front of her. "What's your problem with me, Penny?"

"I don't know what you're talking about," she said.

"You know exactly what I'm talking about," I said.

She started to stare me down but dropped her gaze at the last minute. "I know you don't like me," she finally said.

"Of course I like you," I said.

"You don't have to lie, Daisy," she replied. "I know what everyone thinks of me."

"I *do* like you, Penny," I said.

She gave me a knowing look.

"Most of the time," I amended. "But I thought we had been getting along better lately. Until the past couple of weeks, that is."

"I thought so, too. So why did you say that about me?"

"Why did I say *what* about you?"

"You don't have to deny it," she said. "Ms. Tray told me that you told her I was the least popular person in school."

"Penny, I never said that," I said. "In fact, I don't even talk to Ms. Tray."

"Where are you going right now?"

"To Ms. Tray's office," I said, without thinking.

"You never talk to her, huh?" If possible, Penny looked even madder than before.

"This is the first time I've been to her office," I said. "And besides, I would never say anything like that. Does that sound like me?"

"Not really," she said. "But why would Ms. Tray say something like that?"

"I have no idea," I said. "I know we haven't been the best of friends, but we can try harder."

Penny nodded, but she didn't look like she felt any better.

"The bathroom wall," I said. "That was you, wasn't it?"

She nodded again and looked slightly less tense.

"Why did you do it?" I asked. "*How* did you do it? When did you become a witch?"

"I felt horrible after I did it," she said. "After I saw what the spell did, I tried to fix it, but I couldn't. If I'm a witch, I'm not a very good one."

"It's okay," I said. "My friend Natalie Mason fixed it, but I wouldn't try anything like that again."

"I won't," she promised.

"Maybe I can introduce you to her," I offered. "She might have some pointers for a beginner witch."

"I'd like that," Penny said.

I shifted on my feet, uncertain what to say next. I didn't want to leave. "Hey, do you want to hang out with us at the anniversary party?" I asked.

"Really?" she said. Her face brightened and she smiled for the first time since we'd started talking. "I-I have a date," she confided. "Is it okay if he comes, too?"

"Sure," I said. I wondered who she was going with, but had more pressing concerns. "I've got to go, but I'll see you there."

I hurried off to Ms. Tray's office. I saw Wolfgang Paxton's parents on their way out, looking troubled. Parents talked to guidance counselors all the time. Still, I wondered what kind of advice she'd given the Paxtons.

The door was shut, so I knocked and then tried the door. It was locked.

"Just a moment," Ms. Tray called out. There was a flurry of shuffling papers and then the sound of a drawer *whoosh*ing shut. The door opened and Ms. Tray said, "Please have a seat." She gestured toward a chair full of stuffed pillows. "I'm so glad you could join me," she said.

"Uh, sure," I said. I didn't know why she'd called me into her office, but I'd go along with it.

She didn't say anything else, so I looked around. Her office had been redecorated in early ick. There was a painting of men hunting and killing a unicorn. The decorations on the wall were all vaguely violent, with dripping red hearts and wounded things.

"So Valentine's Day is your favorite holiday?" I asked. I couldn't think of any other reason someone would do that to a perfectly harmless room.

She ignored my comment. "I'm sure you know why I've called you here."

"Not really," I admitted slowly.

"I've been so looking forward to visiting with you," she said. "I've heard so much about you."

"You have?"

"Why of course I have," she said.

"From who?" I folded my arms across my chest.

"That charming young man of yours, and your friends, even your employer," she said.

She'd talked to Slim about me? What did my part-time job have to do with my college education? I'd never heard of a guidance counselor investigating her students.

"You seem to know an awful lot about me," I said.

"Why, of course I do," she said, with a sparkling smile. "It's my job to know everything there is about the students at this school."

"Everything?" I said without thinking. "That seems a little extreme."

Her toothy smile faded. "Everything. Now, about your plans to hold Ryan back by keeping him in Nightshade."

"What?" Her dainty lace gloves were definitely off. "I'm not holding him back," I declared.

"It's just that you two are so attached — it's unhealthy."

"What?" I said, incredulous. "Is that what you told my father?"

"Now, Daisy, part of growing up is letting go."

I wanted to let go of a few choice words. Instead, I stood up. "This meeting is over."

Part of me knew I was behaving badly, but I was beyond caring.

I thought she'd tell me to sit back down or maybe send me to the principal. Instead, she gave me a smile that made my blood freeze.

"I'll decide when it's over," she said.

My response was unintentional. The candy in the bowl on her desk shot into the air like a geyser and then clattered to the floor. I stood there with a hand to my mouth.

What had I done? My abilities weren't exactly a secret, but Ms. Tray was an outsider, and someone I didn't like or trust.

"I'm so sorry," I said. I dropped to the floor and scrambled around to pick up the candy.

"Leave it," she said. "You'll be late for class."

I did as she told me, but as I left, I caught a strange gleam of satisfaction in her eyes.

Great. Instead of a college consultation, I'd made a new enemy. Way to start senior year.

CHAPTER FIFTEEN

During English, I tried to figure out what to tell Ryan. I knew he would ask me about my meeting with Ms. Tray, since he was president of her fan club. He'd already had at least two meetings with her.

"How did your last counseling session go?" I asked Ryan on our way to lunch.

"She's so good at her job," he replied.

"How so?"

"Ms. Tray asked all these questions about my family," he said.

"What kind of questions?"

"Like where my mom was, where my dad grew up, that sort of thing."

"I doubt she was just making conversation," I said. I was sure it was something else. What did Ryan's family have to do with where he went to school? Apart from the financial stuff, of course.

"She's so conscientious," Ryan replied, totally missing my point. "I have another meeting with her next week."

I wasn't too thrilled with the idea of Ryan in another one-on-one session with her. Besides, she was asking way too many questions. And I wanted to know why.

A minute later, a thought slithered through my brain. *They will pay.*

I put a hand to my head as a sharp pain stabbed my temple. The next thing I knew, I was on the floor and Ryan was crouched next to me.

"Daisy, talk to me," he said. "Nurse Phillips will be here in a minute."

The pain in my head was gone, but my mouth felt dry. "I'm okay," I said. I tried to sit up, but Ryan stopped me.

"Don't move until the nurse checks you out."

Nurse Phillips came hurrying toward us. "Daisy, what happened?"

"I . . . fell," I said. "At least, I think that's what happened. I must not have been watching where I was going."

I mean, what else could I say? I wandered into someone else's mind and got a dose of the nasties strong enough to make me faint?

She checked my pulse and shone a light in my eyes. "Let's get you to the infirmary," she said.

Ryan insisted on carrying me. Werewolves were strong, but

I wasn't exactly tiny. He didn't even break out in a sweat. I wrapped my arms around him and held on tight. There were a few strange looks sent our way, but since Nurse Phillips was right behind us, everyone got the picture.

At least, I hoped they did. I saw Penny Edwards texting furiously and hoped it was just a coincidence.

When we reached the nurse's office, Ryan placed me gently on the cot and then stayed with me. He grabbed a chair and pulled it next to me and held my hand. That made me feel much better. Nurse Phillips took my pulse and then got paged to the gym. "I'll be right back," she said.

Samantha came rushing into the nurse's office a few minutes later. "Daisy, I heard you broke your ankle," she said.

"No, I just fell down. I'm fine," I replied.

Ryan snorted. "Typical Nightshade gossip."

I decided I should tell them the truth. If I couldn't be honest with my best friend and boyfriend, who could I be honest with?

"Something weird did happen," I admitted.

"I knew it!" Samantha crowed.

"You don't need to sound so happy about it," I responded.

"Sorry," she said. "Go on."

"I caught someone's thoughts and whoever it was, he or she is full of the most terrible hatred. It gave me a blinding headache. I think I passed out for a minute."

"You didn't pick up anything else?" Ryan said.

I thought about it for a moment. "I'm pretty sure the person was at the school, but other than that, no idea."

Samantha clapped her hands. "A new mystery."

Nurse Phillips came bustling up. Today, her cat's-eyes glasses were purple and her blond beehive was slightly askew. "Daisy, how are you feeling? Do you want me to call your parents?"

"No, I think I can go back to class now," I said. "I'm fine."

She looked at her watch. "You still have time for a bite to eat if you hurry."

Ryan, Sam, and I rushed to the cafeteria, but the selections had been pretty well picked over by the time we got there.

Sean waved us over to his table. "Samantha told me to grab some extra stuff for you guys," he said.

There was a pile of food, including a couple of salads and a giant pizza.

"You're a lifesaver, Sean," I said. My stomach growled and I realized I was starving. Ryan handed me a slice of pizza and a salad.

"Thank you," I said.

We had about fifteen minutes to wolf down the food and get to class. As I chewed my slice, I wondered who at the school had a soul that was as black as licorice and not nearly as tasty.

My headache finally disappeared and I couldn't pick up a trace of the dark thoughts I'd heard earlier. I hurried to my next class. Unfortunately, there was a new headache waiting for me there.

I'd signed up for Nutrition as my elective for fall semester. I liked Ms. Andrews, the teacher, and with my cooking experience, anticipated an easy A. And so far, I'd been getting what I'd signed up for.

But today, I got an unpleasant surprise. Circe Silvertongue was standing next to Ms. Andrews's desk. I smothered a groan and tried to hide behind Tyler Diaz, a six-foot-six basketball player, but no such luck. Circe spotted me and gave me a regal nod.

I was still thinking of ways to get out of class when the bell rang. "Class, settle down, please," Ms. Andrews said. "I have a wonderful surprise for you today. Circe Silvertongue, the executive chef at Wilder's, is here today to give you a cooking lesson."

Wonderful surprise? That's one way to put it. Another would be horrible torture.

"Daisy, come here," Circe commanded. "I require your assistance."

I got up slowly and walked to the front of the room.

"Daisy will act as my assistant," Circe said. "Her cooking skills are adequate."

For the next forty-five minutes, she criticized every single thing I did. Which wasn't exactly new to me, at least not since

I'd started my cooking lessons with her, but I'd never been picked apart in front of my classmates.

We were supposed to be making a simple stir fry, but apparently, even slicing veggies was beyond my meager skills. "Daisy, I said julienne, not enormous clunky hunks," Circe said.

My teeth sank into my bottom lip with the effort of keeping silent and in control of my temper. I wasn't successful, because a decorative pumpkin exploded right next to Circe's head.

The class gasped. Ms. Andrews looked confused. "There must have been something left over from last period's chemistry class," she reasoned. I heaved a sigh of relief.

Circe didn't even seem to notice, until I reached over to brush a chunk of pumpkin out of her hair. The dismissal bell rang right as I finished scraping the last bit of pumpkin into the trash. I had a smear of food across my new white sweater and was hot and sweaty.

"Daisy," Circe called after me as I gathered up my books to make my escape.

"Yes?" Was it possible that she was actually going to pay me a compliment?

No such luck. "Please take that abomination with you when you go."

It was the dish I'd slaved over the entire period. Was she goading me into another pumpkin explosion? I'd give the meal I'd made to Sean, who would eat anything.

CHAPTER SIXTEEN

After school the next day, Ryan called with some upsetting news. When I got off the phone with him, I unloaded my frustrations on my sisters.

"Ryan just got another blackmail note," I stated baldly. "This one asked for money."

I wanted to have a look at the note myself and get some answers, but the moon was full, which meant he wouldn't be around for the rest of tonight or tomorrow. Or answering his cell phone. I'd have to live with my questions for another day.

"Stay calm, Daisy," Rose soothed. "Getting emotional about the situation won't help."

"But it's *Ryan*," I said.

"We know," Rose said. "We know how much he means to you, but you need to stay calm if we're going to be able to help him."

"Who would have a reason to wish Ryan any harm?" Poppy asked.

"That's just it," I said. "I can't think of one single reason. Wolfie's a different story."

"He's a major pain in the butt," Poppy said, nodding her head.

"That reminds me," I said. "I saw his parents coming out of a meeting with the guidance counselor yesterday."

"That woman I met at the fundraiser?" Rose asked. She looked a little disgusted. I was glad I wasn't the only one who was rubbed the wrong way by Ms. Tray. "I wonder if it had anything to do with what I heard from Nicholas."

"What did you hear from Nicholas?" I asked. Since her boyfriend's dad was the head of the Nightshade City Council, he always had the latest gossip on the paranormal community. Especially the shifters, like the Paxton family.

"I heard he withdrew his entire car fund," Rose said. "His parents are furious, but Wolfgang won't tell them what he spent the money on."

My ears prickled. Wolfgang had received a blackmail note, and now he was withdrawing money from the bank? It didn't take a genius to see that the two were related.

"What are his parents going to do?" Poppy asked.

"They're threatening to send him to military school," Rose said.

"Poor Wolfie," I said without thinking.

Poppy gave me a sharp look. "Since when do you have any sympathy for Wolfgang?"

I shrugged. "It just seems a little harsh," I said.

Silence enveloped the room as I made a list of the blackmail victims. Finally I said, "Maybe the blackmail's *not* personal."

"Blackmail's pretty personal," Rose said wryly.

"Blackmail isn't usually just about money," Poppy commented. "It's about having power over someone."

"What do the people on the list have in common?"

We peered down at the list.

Rose snapped her fingers. "They're all paranormals."

Poppy raised an inquiring eyebrow.

I nodded. "I wonder if" — I paused and lowered my voice so Dad wouldn't hear — "the Scourge could be involved."

"Don't worry, Daisy. Dad's upstairs taking a nap," Rose said. "I don't think he can hear you."

"Good," Poppy said. "Because Dad would freak out if it turned out someone from the Scourge was in town! He's already, like, traumatized enough!"

I sighed. She was right. This midday nap was just another example of how Dad's imprisonment at the hands of the Scourge had affected him. His sleeping schedule had been off ever since he'd been back.

"Dad is still being weird about my seeing Ryan," I said.

"You're sneaking around behind Dad's back?" Rose said.

I lifted my chin. "He didn't give me any other choice," I said. "He wouldn't even listen to anything I said about Ryan."

"Well, this isn't helping," she pointed out.

"I seem to recall you snuck out to see Nicholas a few times in your day," Poppy said. She was actually taking my side. Usually my two older sisters sided together.

"Something's got to give soon," I said. "The anniversary ball is next weekend! I can't be grounded for that."

"You should talk to Mom," Poppy suggested.

"She won't help," I said. "She's been tiptoeing around Dad ever since he came home."

"She's doing the best that she can," Rose defended her. "I think you should talk to her."

I sighed. I knew my sisters were right. I went looking for Mom, to have what was sure to be a difficult conversation.

She was home for a change — in the backyard, dead-heading the flowers.

"Mom, you've got to do something about Dad," I said.

She stood up and led me over to the patio table.

"Daisy, why don't you sit down and tell me what's the matter," she said.

"What's the matter?" I said. "Dad is the matter."

"Don't say that," she protested.

"You know it's true," I said. "He's ruining my life. He hovers all the time, he treats me like an infant, and worst of all, he won't let me see Ryan."

"Your dad has had some adjustments to make since he's been back," she said.

"He's not adjusting, that's the problem," I said. "He won't

even give Ryan a chance." I felt tears threatening. "I feel smothered. I'll be in college soon and I can't wait to leave. Because of Dad."

Mom took a long look into my eyes. "Daisy, I know Ryan is a good kid. I shouldn't have let it get so far out of hand. I was just so happy that your father was home that I . . ."

"Didn't want to rock the boat?" I said. "I understand, but I'm a senior, Mom. This is supposed to be the best year of my high school experience. Instead, I'm getting treated like I'm still in elementary school."

"I'll talk to your father. I promise."

I gave a relieved sigh. "Thanks, Mom," I said.

There was motion in the upstairs window, which caught my eye.

My heart sank. My parents' bedroom window, which overlooked the backyard, was open. My father must have woken up and overheard our entire conversation. How was he going to react to the unvarnished truth?

CHAPTER SEVENTEEN

At first, Dad didn't say anything. In fact, I had the feeling he was avoiding me. Not that I could blame him, after all the mean things he'd heard me say. It was the truth, but if I'd known he was listening, I would have been more tactful.

On Thursday he found me in the family room, where I was attempting to study. "I thought I'd make dinner tonight."

"That sounds good," I said cautiously. This was the first conversation we'd had in days.

"Why don't you invite Ryan?" he suggested.

"Ryan? You mean my boyfriend Ryan?"

"Don't sound so surprised," he replied. "Yes, I mean Ryan." I frowned. "What's the catch?"

"There is no catch," he said. He cleared his throat. "I realized I may have been somewhat unreasonable about him. I'd like to have the opportunity to get to know him."

"Dad, you can't treat him the way you have been," I said. "It's not fair."

"I know," he said. "Daisy, I'm trying. I promise I'll behave myself."

I bounded up from the couch and gave him a hug. "Thanks, Dad. I'll call him right now." I was dying to see Ryan, especially since he had just been out of school a few days due to the full moon.

A few hours later, preparations were on their way for a Giordano family dinner.

I followed the delicious smells into the kitchen. "Need any help?"

Dad had gone all out. There was food piled everywhere.

"I've got it handled," he said. "In fact, I may still be able to show you a thing or two, at least in the cooking department. Go get glamorous for that boyfriend of yours," he said, shooing me from the kitchen.

I had to admit it was kind of fun to have someone cooking for me for a change.

Dad had even invited Grandma Giordano to the festivities — I still worried that he planned to feature grilled boyfriend. I knew Ryan could take the heat, but I wasn't sure why Dad disliked him so much.

When Grandma got there, we sat down to dinner. There was silence as everyone appreciated the freshly made pasta and sauce.

"Rafe," Grandma said. "This is delicious. Is it one of my recipes?"

He nodded. "But I did something a little different with the ravioli dough," he said.

"I noticed," she said. "Daisy, your father is the most talented cook I know. You've definitely learned from the best."

"Remember all those cooking lessons, Dad?" I said. "That's one reason I was thinking about going to a culinary institute after college."

He beamed, clearly pleased, and then changed the subject.

"How's your father, Ryan?" Dad asked.

"Busy," Ryan said. "That blackmail case is keeping him awake nights."

I kicked him under the table. We didn't tell my dad about the awful things that occasionally happened in Nightshade, because we didn't want him to worry.

My father didn't comment, but asked another question. "Do you and your father get along well?"

Ryan didn't even flinch. "My dad is great," he said loyally. "I couldn't ask for a better father."

Dad's expression softened. If the question had been some sort of test, it was obvious that Ryan had passed with flying colors.

"Ryan, why don't you help me with the dishes?"

"I'll help, too," I said quickly.

My dad smiled but shook his head. "I'd like to get to know your young man a bit better."

I gave Mom an imploring look, but she only smiled placidly.

Do something, I sent a silent plea to Rose.

Don't worry, she told me. *Dad won't hurt him.*

"Cut it out," Poppy said. She'd caught us in our silent communication. I think it bothered her that Rose and I both had the power of telepathy.

Ryan and Dad came back about ten minutes later. My dad was smiling broadly, which wasn't necessarily a good sign. Ryan's face was noncommittal.

"Who's up for coffee?" Mom asked, with what I thought was totally inappropriate cheerfulness.

"I'll get it," Poppy said.

"I'll help," I said.

Once in the kitchen, I moaned. "This is a disaster."

"You're making a big deal of nothing," she said.

"I'll remember that when he corners *your* boyfriend," I said. I could have bitten my tongue when I saw the stricken look on her face. Her last boyfriend, Gage, a ghost, had vanished on the dance floor at prom.

"I'm so sorry," I said. "Me and my big mouth."

She gave me a tiny smile. "It's okay," she said. "At least you and Rose aren't tiptoeing around me anymore. I've actually been thinking about dating again."

I must have looked dubious, because she said, "No, really, I am. Thinking about it, I mean. I don't think I'm ready for an actual date yet, but I'm getting there."

"That's great," I replied. She'd been pretty devastated about

Gage and until recently, her notebooks were covered with sad doodles of Gage and Poppy forever. Lately, though, her notebooks were pristine, which I took as a sign that she might be ready to fall in love again.

Mom came into the kitchen. "What's taking you girls so long?" she asked.

"Just a little chat," I said. "We'll be out in a minute."

"You'd better hurry," Mom warned. "Your father is getting out the family photos."

I groaned. "We'll hurry." The last thing I needed was Ryan and Dad bonding over my baby pictures.

I got out cups while Poppy got out the cream, sugar, and flavored syrups. "What flavor does Ryan like?" she asked. "We have hazelnut, vanilla, and almond."

"Just bring a little of everything," I said. "And hurry."

We rushed back to the living room, where everything appeared to be running smoothly. There wasn't any sign of my baby book, but I saw Mom slip something into a drawer when Dad wasn't looking.

"You are the best mom ever," I told her.

She leaned in and gave me a hug. "You'd better distract your father before he remembers the home movies," she whispered.

"Ryan has been telling me about your recent adventures," my dad said.

"Really?" I sent a panicked look at my mom, but she only smiled serenely.

"It sounds like you can think on your feet," Dad said.

"Daisy does think fast," Poppy agreed. "Like the time there was this soul-sucking vampire who was targeting the cheerleaders and she . . ." She trailed off when she saw Dad's face.

Definitely too much information. It was time to change the subject.

"So, I'm halfway through my lessons with Circe now," I said.

"I'll bet that's some relief," Poppy said.

"Yeah," I admitted. "She's tough to work with, but I have been learning a lot."

"Between those cooking lessons and the anniversary preparations, you've been spending a lot of time up at the Wilder place," Grandma noted. "Have you seen much of Mrs. Wilder?"

"Not really," I said. "But she's been great about letting us borrow old furniture from storage to use at the Nightshade Through the Ages ball. Isn't that nice of her?"

"That's very nice of her."

I turned to Mom. "I want to help her find her sister," I said. "She's never given up hope. Like you never gave up looking for Dad, never believed those awful things people said."

I glanced at Dad when I said it. Mom hadn't ever given up, hadn't stopped looking for him. Even when there were rumors that he'd left her for another woman.

My parents were loyal to each other, no matter what.

Mom gave Dad's hand a squeeze and her eyes were misty.

"Mom, I didn't mean to make you cry," I said.

"No, Daisy, it's fine," she said. She cleared your throat. "But you're right. I *would* want to know. As soon as the opportunity presents itself, I will ask Mrs. Wilder if I can help find her sister."

"We'll help, too," Rose said. "If we can."

The entire table turned to Dad, waiting for his response.

"As long as you're careful," he said.

We all cheered and he blushed profusely. "Who would like dessert?" he said. "I made red velvet cake. It's your mother's favorite." He turned to her and said anxiously, "It's still your favorite, isn't it?"

She gave him a kiss. "Of course it is. Red velvet cake made by my husband. There's nothing I'd rather have."

It was so sweet that the entire table had to look away.

Finally, Grandma Giordano said, "Where's that cake you promised us, Rafe?"

We all laughed.

Mom and Dad went to the kitchen to get the cake. They were gone a long time and when they came back, Mom was giggling and Dad had a smudge of lipstick on his shirt.

I dug into my dessert and tried not to think about it. After dessert, Rose and Poppy volunteered to clean up.

My mom smothered a yawn and Ryan got to his feet a minute later.

"Thank you for a wonderful evening," Ryan said politely. "But it's getting late. I should be going."

"I'll walk you out," I said. I crossed my fingers that Dad wouldn't object.

He didn't. He gave me a smile. "Have fun."

As soon as we were out the door, Ryan took my hand. "Thanks for inviting me to dinner," he said.

"Thanks for coming," I said. Ryan took a seat on the porch swing and pulled me into his lap and gave me a gentle kiss.

"It's such a relief," Ryan said. "I couldn't stand the thought that your dad didn't like me."

"Me, too," I said. "But everything is all right now."

He kissed me again, and for that moment, everything was more than all right. Everything was perfect.

CHAPTER EIGHTEEN

Things were winding down as far as Nightshade's anniversary. I was scheduled for one more volunteer session for the big party. I pulled up to the Wilder estate, prepared to spend the day at Sam's beck and call.

Jordan and Rachel were sitting on the floor and a tarp was spread out in front of them. They were painting a large mural of cartoony ghosts, goblins, and witches.

"For the kids' tables," Jordan explained. "Samantha didn't want anything too scary for them."

I understood the theory, even though some of the toddlers who lived in Nightshade were more frightening than any of Sam's scariest decorations.

"I brought snacks," I said, and held up a pan of brownies. "This is the recipe Circe said wasn't up to her standards."

"That's not very nice!" Jordan said.

They each grabbed a brownie and bit into it.

Samantha approached and grabbed one for herself. "These

are delicious. Circe doesn't know what she's talking about." She took a delicate nibble and stared into space. I knew that look.

"In fact," she said. "Would you help me finalize the menu for the dance?"

"Isn't Circe catering it?" Rachel asked.

"Most of it," Sam said. "She's serving a bunch of fancy stuff. But I want something that the kids will actually eat."

"Why not ask Slim to cater burgers and fries? He could use the business."

"That's a great idea," Samantha said. "The city council wants the dance to be for everybody in Nightshade, not just the adults."

It seemed like just about everything was in place for the anniversary party, except for one thing. What was I going to wear? In the last few weeks I'd been so preoccupied, I hadn't even thought about it. But Samantha had a surprise for me.

"I found the perfect dress for you!" she said. "Come see." Samantha wasn't psychic, but sometimes she could read my mind.

She dragged me to another storage room, where trunks in all shapes and sizes were scattered throughout. There was also a large mahogany armoire pushed into the corner, and that's where Sam headed.

She pulled out a couple of dresses. "I thought I'd wear this one," she said, holding up a black flapper gown.

"It looks really old," I said. "Like it belongs in a museum

somewhere. Are you sure Mrs. Wilder won't mind?"

"I asked her and she said it was fine to borrow whatever we could find in storage," she said.

"You'll be gorgeous," I said. The black beaded silk dress would be perfect with Samantha's pale hair.

She danced a little jig. "I know," she said. "But wait until you see *your* dress."

She dug through the armoire until she found what she was looking for. She held out a lavender and white dress, which looked vaguely Victorian in style. It was beautiful, but something made me say, "It's gorgeous, Sam, but can I see what else is in there?"

She stepped aside, not at all disappointed that I didn't want to commit to the dress she'd picked out for me.

I stuck my head into the armoire. It was bursting with clothing from the past. I hesitated in front of a long slinky thirties gown of white satin but kept looking.

An hour later, I'd made my way to the very back of the armoire and had almost given up. I was hot and sweaty and covered with dust and I didn't know what else.

There was one last dress hanging in the back. When I touched its sleeve, a zing went through me and I knew I'd found what I was looking for.

I pulled it out carefully.

Sam looked at me. "It's made for you," she said.

I sucked in my breath. "You can't be serious," I said. "I can't wear that. It can't possibly fit me."

"Try it on," Samantha urged.

I touched the gossamer fabric. "Okay," I said. I folded it over my arm and carefully carried it to where there was better light. The thought of getting even a speck of dust on it made me queasy.

It was midnight blue, with a square bodice and an ivory satin underskirt. There were little silk flowers at the waist and ivory embroidery at the wrists and hem.

I couldn't bear to let that gorgeous dress out of sight.

"Hurry back," Samantha said.

Instead, I got lost. In my defense, the Wilder place was huge and full of empty corridors and twisting staircases and rooms that led nowhere.

I finally found a bathroom and slipped in to clean up. I tried on the dress, holding my breath until it slid on. It fit like it was made for me.

I wadded up the clothes I'd been wearing and headed in the direction I thought would lead me back to Sam. Instead, I came face-to-face with Mrs. Wilder.

"Is it really you?" she said. "Lily?"

"Mrs. Wilder? I'm sorry I startled you," I said. "It's Daisy. Daisy Giordano."

"You looked so much like her for a moment," she said. "And that dress. Where did you find it?"

"Like who?" I asked. "Who do I look like?" But she didn't answer.

She held out a hand and touched the soft fabric of the dress. "She was so young and in love," she said softly.

"Who was?"

"Someone I knew a very long time ago," Mrs. Wilder said. She was lost in thought and I stood rooted to the spot, not sure if I should leave or just wait for her to say something else. Finally, she sighed and seemed to recall where she was.

"Samantha said it was okay for me to borrow this for the anniversary party," I said. I gestured toward the gown, secretly praying that she wouldn't order me to take it off immediately.

She smiled. "You look lovely in the dress, Daisy," she said. "Please wear it and have a magical night."

"Mrs. Wilder, thank you so much. It's such a beautiful gown."

Her expression sharpened and she changed the subject abruptly. "Bianca tells me that you've been getting cooking lessons from Circe as part of some contest."

"Yes, ma'am, I have," I said. I didn't know what else to say.

"You enjoy cooking?" she said, clearly perplexed by the idea.

"I really do," I replied.

"I never learned," she said. "And Circe has been kind to you?"

I hesitated, not sure what to say and finally settled on a polite phrase. "I've been learning a lot."

"Hmph," she said. "I expect a clever girl like you knows to be on guard with Circe Silvertongue. But if you have any difficulties, please come see me at once."

"I will," I promised. "But why would you . . ." My voice trailed off as soon as I remembered I was talking to the matriarch of the most powerful shifter family in town. Even her granddaughter Elise scared me.

"Why would I hire someone as volatile as Circe? Because everyone deserves a second chance," she said softly.

I met her eyes for a moment, but then shied away from the depths of knowledge I saw in them.

"Well, thanks again for the dress," I said. I backed away and then practically ran to find Samantha.

Wandering the halls of the Wilder estate could be hazardous to your health. Or at least to your peace of mind.

Sam was in the room we used as our anniversary party headquarters. She was standing in front of the portrait of the young woman we had seen earlier.

"What are you doing with that?" I asked.

"I want to bring it over to Merriweather House," she said. "It'll be perfect over the marble fireplace."

"It will look great there," I said.

"Did you notice anything else?" she asked.

"She's wearing my dress!" I said. "I mean, the dress I'm borrowing for the party."

"Exactly," she said. "I think we should style your hair like she's wearing it in the painting."

"I think I will," I said. I took another long look at the girl and then flipped the painting over. Lily was written on the back. The name hadn't really registered before. Lily, the name Mrs. Wilder had called me. Her sister.

A shiver traveled down my spine. There was something creepy about wearing Lily's dress.

CHAPTER NINETEEN

It was finally Halloween, and the anniversary party. Slim had assured me several times that he could handle the kids' buffet. "Go have fun," he said. I canceled my cooking lesson with Circe that day, knowing it would just turn into indentured servitude. Slim was right. I needed a day to just kick back and have fun.

I took one more look in the mirror. The blue and ivory gown suited my coloring, and Poppy had managed to style my hair in an approximation of the girl's in the painting.

I wore ivory ballet flats and simple gold jewelry. Silver was out of the question, at least if I wanted to slow dance with my boyfriend.

Samantha was absolutely gorgeous in the black flapper dress. She twirled around and the crystal beads sparkled as she moved. "What do you think?"

"You're stunning," I said.

"Not so bad yourself," she said. We exchanged smiles.

We had to be at Merriweather House early, even though a

bunch of women from the garden club had volunteered to do setup.

"Is your dad coming tonight?" I asked her as we prepared for the big evening. I didn't ask about her mother, who rarely came to Nightshade since the divorce.

She made a face. "Yes, and he's bringing a date."

"A date?" I don't know why it came as a shock. Sam's parents had been apart for a long time and the women of Nightshade seemed to think he looked like George Clooney. "With who?"

"He won't tell me. Says he wants it to be a surprise."

Mom knocked on the door. "Daisy, the boys are here."

"We'll be down in a minute, Mom," I said.

I stuck my head out my door. "Poppy, we're leaving now. Are you coming with us?" I called out.

"No thanks," she replied. "I'm still getting ready. I've got a ride, so you guys go ahead."

She was probably riding with Nicholas and Rose. I hoped Poppy would find a new guy soon. I worried that she was still moping over Gage.

I spritzed on a little perfume and Samantha primped a few minutes longer. Then she sat down on the bed.

"Aren't you ready?" I asked.

"We need to make an entrance," she said.

I grabbed her by the hand and pulled her up. "The heck with an entrance," I said. "I want to see my boyfriend."

Ryan and Sean both wore plain black tuxedos, paired with snowy white shirts. But when I leaned up to give my boyfriend a kiss, I noticed his tie. It was a plain dark black, but a spider dangling from a web was embroidered into the fabric.

"Nice tie," I said. I smoothed my hand over the fabric.

He grinned at me. "I needed something festive for Halloween and Sam vetoed the pumpkin ties."

That's when I noticed that Sean had on the same exact tie.

"That's a relief," I said.

"Have I told you how gorgeous you look?" Ryan said. "That dress is amazing."

"I know, huh?" Samantha said. "She's devastating in that dress."

"We're going to be devastatingly late if we don't get a move-on," I pointed out, uncomfortable with the compliment fest coming from my best friend and boyfriend.

The ballroom was tastefully, yet festively, decorated in deep purple, white, and black. Tall candelabra flanked the buffet table, and fairy lights twinkled from every available pillar and piece of greenery. The entire population of Nightshade, the normal and the paranormal, were out in full force, the women in long gowns and the men in tuxedos or suits.

There were several round tables set with white linens, fancy china, and fine cutlery. There wasn't anything silver in the room, as a courtesy to the Were residents in Nightshade.

"Samantha, you did a fantastic job," I said.

"I was going for eerily elegant," she said.

"You succeeded," I said. "It's creepy cool."

I spotted the pile of sugar skulls that I'd slaved over, next to a large crystal punch bowl filled with some mysterious brew, which was steaming. Dry ice. Probably.

"You don't know how hard it was to make sure we didn't have any silver around," Sam said. "Or garlic."

"Is that true — that vampires can't stand garlic?"

She shrugged. "I wasn't going to find a vampire to ask, but I didn't want to take the chance."

Sean said, "C'mon, let's find a table. I'm hungry."

"You're always hungry," Samantha said.

"Kids' buffet or adult?" I said to Ryan.

"Are you kidding?" he said. "I'll take Slim's over Circe's cooking any day."

"Shh, not too loud," I said. But secretly I agreed with him.

Slim and Natalie were working the buffet. Natalie wore a simple dark green dress, and Slim wore a long-sleeved tuxedo T-shirt and black tuxedo pants and had a long black scarf wrapped around his neck. A black fedora was pulled down low over where his face would normally be, and he wore black gloves, to serve the food. If you didn't look too closely, you might not even notice he was invisible.

He caught me staring at his shirt. "Shh, it's Flo's," he said. "I borrowed it for tonight."

"And he better not get anything on it, either," Flo said.

She was standing next to me, wearing what looked to be a fortune in diamonds. Her hair was piled high, and she wore a long white satin dress from the forties.

"You like it?" she asked. The front of the dress was modest, but when she twirled, the back of the dress was bare, falling to a puddle at the curve of her spine. Her tattoos swirled and danced to the music.

"You're breathtaking," her date said. It was Vinnie Leon. The drummer from Side Effects May Vary looked very dapper in his red shirt, checkered pants, suspenders, and spats.

I glanced at the fifties room, not far from Slim's buffet, and noticed a familiar-looking shape.

"Is that . . . ?" I said, pointing to the item in the corner.

"The one and only," Flo said. It was Lil, spinning singles appropriate for a sock hop. "Samantha asked to borrow her, to add some authenticity to the fifties room."

"Sounds like she's still upset about something," I said, recognizing the pouty song "Party Lights" by little Claudine Clark blaring from the side room.

"I don't know why," Slim said. "She should feel right at home at Merriweather House. I bought her at an estate sale here."

I was stunned by this news, but before I had time to ask Slim more questions, we were interrupted by Penny and her date. I almost didn't recognize her. She wore a simple long white dress with gold embroidery on the hem and bodice. It was head and shoulders above the kind of outfit Penny usually wore.

"Penny, you look amazing," I said.

"Really?" she said shyly. "It was my grandma's dress."

"You're gorgeous," Sam affirmed. "Tyler certainly seems to think so."

"Thanks," Penny said, blushing prettily. Her date was Tyler, from my nutrition class.

Penny was carrying the La Contessa bag, and I took the opportunity to grill her about it. "I love your purse," I said. "Where did you get it? It looks expensive."

She giggled. "You wouldn't believe where I got it."

"Where?" I said, holding my breath.

"The swap meet," she said. "It's a copycat. But don't tell anyone."

Tyler didn't say much, but he grinned the entire time. He was clearly pleased to be Penny's escort for the evening.

We saw Mom and Dad as we headed back to get a table. I waved and they made their way over to us. He shook hands with Ryan. My father was making an effort, but I could tell he still wasn't comfortable with the fact that I was in a serious relationship.

Ryan picked up on my dad's mood and quickly offered to get my parents some punch.

Dad wore a white dinner jacket and black trousers and my mother looked absolutely dazzling in a simple black sheath and classic pearls.

"Very Jackie O," Sam said approvingly.

"Who's Jackie O?" Sean said.

Sam shook her head in despair at her boyfriend's lack of historical fashion sense.

"Think you can spare a burger for your dad?" my father asked me.

"What's wrong with your meal?" I said. "Circe trained at the Cordon Bleu."

"There's nothing *wrong* with it," Dad said. "I just don't want to eat her food." He shuddered theatrically. "There are truffles in practically everything."

I put a burger on his plate and then added some fries. "Okay, but you owe me," I said.

Mom giggled, but Dad gave me a grateful smile. "You're my favorite daughter."

"You say that to all of us," I reminded him.

Ryan came back with the punch.

"Thank you, Ryan," Mom said. Then to Dad, she said, "Let's leave these kids alone. I see the garden club chairperson and I need to say hi."

Later, after we'd stuffed ourselves on Slim's delicious food, we took a stroll outside. Ryan took every opportunity to find dark corners and kiss me senseless.

When we got back, the tables had been cleared away, to make room for dancing, and a tuxedoed band (not Side Effects May Vary, unfortunately) was setting up its instruments.

Rose and Nicholas arrived, wearing late-1800s period costumes. Her dress was pale pink and was trimmed with white silk roses.

Poppy was with them and evidently had a date. She wore a short black dress that looked like it was made sometime in the eighties, with black heels adorned with red satin bows.

Her date loitered in the background, but I saw her put out a hand and touch his arm once. I couldn't wait to get her alone and ask her who he was.

Mr. Devereaux walked into the ballroom. He looked dapper in a designer tux, but it was the woman clinging to his arm who made me stop and stare.

I nudged Sam. "Your dad brought *Ms. Tray?*"

She winced. "That's his surprise?" she asked in a whisper. "She scares me."

"Me, too," I said.

"Who is that with your dad?" Poppy asked Sam.

"Our guidance counselor," Samantha explained.

"Isn't she just the cutest little thing?" Rose said sarcastically, in a fake southern drawl.

"She's the bane of my existence," I said. "She's the one who had a chat with Dad about my future."

"Isn't that her job?" Poppy replied.

"Not the way she does it," I said. "That's what made him ground me!"

Just then Dad approached our group. "You kids talking

about me?" he asked. Then he saw where we were looking, and he said, "Hey, isn't that —"

Ms. Tray wore a shiny red micro-mini dress and white go-go boots. Definitely not the best look for the over thirty crowd. Her hair was teased to the sky, and it looked like she had killed a couple of black widows and plastered them on her eyes.

"Rafe," she trilled at my father. "What a pleasure to see y'all here. When Spenser told me you were old friends, I couldn't wait to come to this event."

Mr. Devereaux and my dad did one of those half hug/half handshake things that guys did.

"Her southern accent is slipping," Sam observed.

"Her accent is as phony as she is," I replied.

We turned our attention back to the grownups' conversation. Ms. Tray still had the floor, and even my mother looked a trifle impatient.

My father muttered something unintelligible, but it didn't slow the counselor down.

"Spenser has done such an excellent job with Sabrina. I thought you could get the two girls together. Sabrina could be such a positive influence on Daisy."

Even Mr. Devereaux rolled his eyes at that one. The guidance counselor was obviously clueless.

"*Samantha*"—Mr. Devereaux emphasized his daughter's name —"and Daisy have been friends since grade school."

Ms. Tray eventually caught on that nobody was buying her concerned act. "Well," she said lamely. "Isn't that nice?"

"Yes, it is," my father said. "We're very proud of both the girls."

"But —" Ms. Tray started to say something, but Mr. Devereaux gently pulled her away and onto the dance floor.

Dad stared after them. "That woman is a menace."

"I couldn't agree more," Mom said, returning from her chat with the garden club members. "Now, come dance with me." She took his hand and they joined the other dancers.

Ryan took me by the hand and spun me around. "Feel like dancing?"

"I'd love to," I said.

There was a big commotion when Circe came out, still in her white chef's jacket, to mingle with the crowd. Someone started clapping until everyone joined in.

Circe took a low bow, but then straightened abruptly when she saw me. She strode over and grabbed my arm. "Where did you get that dress?" she said.

I twisted my arm away from her. "Mrs. Wilder said I could borrow it," I said. "Why do you care?"

Her eyes turned a furious green and I took a step back. She started to say something, but then noticed that everyone was watching her. She forced a smile. "You look . . . lovely," she said through clenched teeth.

At that moment, the bandleader announced that they were taking a break. With one last glare, Circe returned to the kitchen.

I was shaken by my confrontation with Circe. I retreated to the fifties room with Ryan and fed Lil a quarter. A song I'd never heard before came on. It was simply piano music, in a plunking, upbeat melody.

Mr. Todeschi, Nightshade High's band instructor, was also in the room. His face lit up and his toe tapped in time to the music.

"Do you know what song this is?" I asked him.

"Why, it's a Scott Joplin rag," he said.

"What?" I had no idea what he was talking about.

"It was written in the early 1900s," he explained.

"Do you know the name of it?" Ryan said.

"Let me think," Mr. Todeschi said. "It'll come to me in a minute."

We were all quiet while he tried to remember. Lil had to have a reason to play the song.

He snapped his fingers. "I've got it. I'm pretty sure it's 'Lily Queen.'"

"*Lily Queen*"? Lily was the name of the girl in the painting. Mrs. Wilder's sister.

Balthazar came trotting in. He seemed to be drawn to the music. His tail moved in time to the music. He went up to the jukebox and nuzzled it with his nose.

Lil shimmied and shook. I thought I saw a faint form of a woman floating in the air, next to the jukebox, but before I could say anything to Ryan, it disappeared. It must have been a trick of the candlelight or something.

The next song she played was Whitney Houston's rendition of "I Will Always Love You." The pig made snuffling noises, which sounded like great noisy sobs.

The jukebox went silent and then Circe's voice came from the direction of the kitchen.

"Balthazar, where are you?" she practically screamed.

The pig cringed but stayed where he was.

Circe stormed into the room. Her green eyes sent sparks all over the room, and I took a step back into the protection of Ryan's arms.

She started toward Balthazar and the pig ran around the room, squealing frantically as he went.

"Roast pork is on the menu tomorrow," she announced in a menacing voice.

All the noise in the room ceased. Circe was threatening to roast Balthazar, who was, granted, a pig, but one that Circe had babied and treated like a pet. You simply didn't eat your pets, not even in Nightshade.

She had him cornered and the pig's legs shook in fear. She raised her arm as if to strike him, but a voice stopped her.

Mr. Bone stepped forward. "Circe Silvertongue, you will not harm Balthazar," he said. "The council overlooked the unfortunate result of your lack of control once, but you must live with the consequences."

She froze, her muscles straining with the effort. Finally, she choked out, "But —"

"There are no *buts*," he said sternly. "You will continue to look after that pig and insure his continued good health. There are rumors of your involvement in certain events."

"That is just a rumor," she cried.

"Let me finish," he scolded her.

"Yes, sir," she said meekly.

He continued, "If any concrete evidence comes to the council's attention, there will be grave consequences. Do I make myself clear?"

The pig seemed to gather his courage. He threw Circe a clearly defiant look before he trotted over to the jukebox and nuzzled Lil. He then left the ballroom without waiting to see Circe's reaction.

The jukebox responded with a song. "You Are the Best Thing" by Ray LaMontagne came on.

Clearly chastened, Circe followed the pig back into the kitchen. The crowd returned its attention to the celebration.

Mr. Devereaux and Ms. Tray didn't look like they were having much fun. He wasn't responding to her flirtatious smiles and she was clearly miffed about it.

"I don't get why she hates me so much and likes you," I said to Ryan.

"Maybe she's into Ryan," Sean offered.

I stopped in my tracks. "You think she doesn't like me because she's *jealous?*"

He shrugged. "It's something," he said. "She's always pretty nice to me."

"Me, too," Samantha said. "But there is something kind of off about her."

Sean opened his mouth, but Samantha silenced him with one look. "And I'm *not* saying that because she's after my dad," she said.

"That's a repulsive thought," I said.

"Yes, it is," she said. "Be glad that your parents are so incredibly devoted." She gestured toward the dance floor, where my parents were still dancing, completely oblivious of everyone around them.

I nestled closer to Ryan, content. All my family and friends were there and we were having a truly magical night. Everything else could wait until the morning.

CHAPTER TWENTY

I was looking for Poppy and I finally spotted her heading into the 1920s room.

"Excuse me," I said to Ryan. "I want to talk to Poppy for a minute."

"I'll get us some punch," Ryan replied.

The twenties room was decorated like a jazz club, complete with art deco posters, gilt mirrors, and a jazz combo. I could see Poppy across the room, but there was no sign of her date. As I walked over to her, I noticed that Mr. Bone and some of the council members were conferring about something in the corner.

Poppy was sitting on a velvet sofa and I sat down next to her.

"Are you having fun?" I asked her.

She smiled. "I am."

"Who is that guy you're with?" I asked.

She giggled. "I knew you'd be over here. It's a setup," she

explained. "He's a friend of Nicholas's and he's a junior at UC Nightshade. He seems nice."

There was an unspoken *but* in there somewhere. Still, it was good that she was finally dating again.

Her date returned, hovering bashfully in the background until Poppy introduced us.

"This is Liam."

"Nice to meet you," he said to me.

"You, too." I was trying to think of something interesting to say. "Poppy said you go to UC Nightshade. Do you live on campus?"

He looked at his shoes. "No, I live with some friends off campus."

His teeth were incredibly white, and for a minute, I thought I saw a hint of fangs. But there were no other signs that he was a vampire. It must have been my imagination.

I excused myself and went to find Samantha. She was chatting with her father and Ms. Tray. Samantha had a pained look on her face. Mr. Devereaux looked embarrassed. Obviously, his date was not going well. They left early, and the evening became a lot more fun without Ms. Tray watching my every move.

Ryan and Sean came back with cups of punch and the four of us drifted away.

"So what now?" Samantha said.

"Now I want to dance with my boyfriend," I said. I took Ryan's hand.

"What about your dad?" he asked.

"We've come to an agreement," I said. "He promised not to treat me like I'm twelve and I promised not to scare the heck out of him anymore."

I pointed to where he was slow-dancing with Mom. They both had blissed-out expressions on their faces. "Besides, he looks pretty occupied."

Ryan pulled me close and whispered against my hair. "I'm glad your dad changed his mind about me."

"I am, too," I said. I twined my arms around his neck and looked up at him. "Now can we stop talking about my dad?"

Ryan's answer was a long slow kiss. When I could breathe again, I realized that the music had stopped and Mr. Bone was standing in front of the band with a microphone in his hand.

"Nightshade citizens, your votes have been counted. It gives me great pleasure to announce the king and queen of the Midnight Ball," he said. "Samantha Devereaux and Sean Walsh."

Ryan let out a piercing whistle, but Samantha and Sean weren't paying attention, not at first. They were gazing into each other's eyes, completely oblivious to Mr. Bone calling their names and to the cheering crowd.

Finally, the noise registered and Samantha raised her head and looked over at me, completely puzzled.

Mr. Bone cleared his throat. "Samantha Devereaux and Sean Walsh, please join me onstage," he said.

Samantha rushed to the stage, got halfway there and realized Sean was still standing in the spot where she'd left him. She went back for her boyfriend, took his hand, and led him to where Mr. Bone stood.

The crowd broke into another round of applause. After Mr. Bone handed Sam a giant bouquet of flowers and set a tiara on her head, Sean led Samantha back onto the dance floor.

My best friend was radiant as she rested her head on her boyfriend's shoulder.

"Samantha looks beautiful tonight," a voice said behind me.

It was Mrs. Wilder's granddaughter, Elise. She wore a killer red silk gown that had to be designer. "Elise, it's nice to see you here," I said. "How's college?" Elise was a freshman at UCLA.

"College is great. I'm just back for the weekend. I couldn't miss the anniversary party," she said.

"Is Bane here, too?" Bane Paxton was Elise's boyfriend and Wolfgang's older brother.

She gestured to the dance floor. "He's dancing with Gran," she said.

Bane was doing a careful waltz with Mrs. Wilder.

"She looks like she's having fun," I said.

"Keep an eye on her for me, Daisy," Elise said. "She's getting pretty fragile and I worry about her when I'm gone." She paused, then said, "Don't tell Gran, but I'm thinking of transferring back to UC Nightshade next semester."

I remembered what my mom had told me about the Wilder family tragedy. Approaching a shifter was dicey, anyway, and Elise made me nervous at the best of times.

"I heard about what happened to her sister," I said.

"And?" Elise's face was unreadable.

"You may have heard that my mom is a psychic investigator?"

"Go on," she said.

"Mom thought that she — that we — might be able to help find out what happened to your grandmother's sister."

"It's nice of you to offer, but I don't think so," Elise said. "Grandmother gets upset whenever she hears Lily's name mentioned."

I remembered the faraway look in Mrs. Wilder's eye.

"I think you should let us try," I said stubbornly. "Wouldn't you want to know? Maybe it will give her some peace."

Elise finally nodded. "You have my permission," she said. "But not a word to my grandmother."

"How am I supposed to get any information? Mom needs a piece of clothing or something."

"That part's easy," Elise said. "You're wearing the gown Lily wore the night before she disappeared."

"One last thing," I said. "Do you by any chance know Bam's real name?"

"I do," she said. "I saw it on the engagement announcement in Grandmother's scrapbook once. They'd already sent the notice to the paper. His nickname came from the first letters of his name. Balthazar Anthony Merriweather. B-A-M."

Balthazar? Like the pig? An idea started niggling at my brain.

The song ended and Bane escorted Mrs. Wilder to a chair nearby, which ended my conversation with Elise.

Ryan came up and swept me into his arms and onto the dance floor. Just as the last song faded away, it finally hit me.

I stopped and looked up at him. "I know what happened to Bam and Lily!" I said. But before I could tell Mrs. Wilder, I needed to be sure.

CHAPTER TWENTY-ONE

Sunday morning, I waited until it wasn't hazardous to my health to call Sam.

"Can you still get into Merriweather House?" I asked. "I need to look around."

"We have cleanup crews there today," she said. She smothered a yawn. "Why didn't you look around last night?"

"There were too many people there," I said. "It would have made someone suspicious."

"You are too mysterious this early in the morning," Sam said. "Give me an hour and I'll go with you."

Fortunately, neither of my sisters were awake yet, so I nabbed the car we shared. I picked Sam up at her house and explained my theory on the way.

"You think Circe turned someone into a pig?" Sam said doubtfully.

"It all fits," I insisted. "The pen engraved with his initials, her pet pig Balthazar, everything."

"She's a lot younger than Mrs. Wilder," Sam said.

"No, she's not," I explained. "She only *looks* younger. She's a sorceress, remember? How hard would it be to glam things up a bit?"

"Why would Mrs. Wilder hire her, then?"

"Because she had no idea that Circe was behind her sister's disappearance. Of course."

Merriweather House looked pretty deserted, but I noticed my grandma's car.

"So what now?" Sam asked.

"I need to look on the second floor. Is it safe?"

"Yes," she said. "Mrs. Wilder asked me not to let anyone upstairs because some of her sister's personal items are stored up there."

"Jackpot," I said.

"What are you looking for?" Sam asked.

"I don't know," I said. "Something that will tie Circe Silvertongue to Lily and her fiancé."

Grandma had been a fountain of useful information previously. Maybe she'd be of some help now, if I jogged her memory just a bit.

We found her on a ladder in the ballroom. She was taking down decorations. There were a dozen or so clear plastic containers stacked up near her, but there wasn't another soul in the room.

"Grandma, you shouldn't be on a ladder all alone in this house," I scolded her.

"Oh, goodness, you startled me," she said. "And Edna is in the other room, making a pot of coffee."

She came down from the ladder. "What are you girls doing here so early? I thought you'd still be sleeping."

"We have a favor to ask you," I said. "Do you remember anything about Circe Silvertongue in conjunction with Lily and Bam Merriweather?"

"Sure," she said. "I was a lot younger than they were, of course," she added archly. "But everyone knew that Circe had set her cap for Bam, but he wasn't interested. Not in anything serious, anyway. Then he met Lily and he never looked at anyone else."

"Thanks, Grandma," I said. I kissed her cheek. "You don't know how much help you've been."

I grabbed Sam's arm. "C'mon, let's go talk to Mr. Bone," I said. "He'll know what to do. I'm not stupid enough to confront a sorceress without backup."

Mr. Bone wasn't at the mortuary, but I put in a call to Nicholas, who told me his father was on the golf course.

"Can you have him meet us at Slim's?" I asked. "It's important."

"I can't make any promises," he said. "You know how Dad is about getting in his eighteen holes."

"Tell him it's about Mrs. Wilder's sister, Lily," I said.

Nicholas promised he would and we hung up.

"What now?" Sam said.

"Now I buy you a cup of coffee," I replied.

We sat at a booth and ordered coffee and a couple of cinnamon rolls and waited. Samantha was texting Sean, but I couldn't sit still or concentrate on anything.

Mr. Bone hurried in. "Daisy, Nicholas said it was important."

"It is," I said. Sam and I told him my theory about Balthazar while Mr. Bone ordered and ate two cinnamon rolls and drank an enormous cup of coffee.

"Hmm," he said. "Daisy, I think you're on to something," he said. "But I'm afraid you're too late."

"What?" I cried.

"Circe Silvertongue left Nightshade last night, right after the party. And she took Balthazar."

My jaw dropped open. It was bad enough that she was taking Bam away from Lily again, but she also still owed me four more cooking lessons.

"I'm afraid it's true," he replied. "The council has been investigating the possibility that Circe was responsible for the disappearance of Bam Merriweather. We believe that there is evidence somewhere tying Circe to Lily's disappearance, as well."

"What now?"

"Circe is a public figure. She can run, but she can't hide. I'm confident we will be able to find the evidence tying her to Lily's disappearance and then bring Circe back to Nightshade to mete out justice."

I shivered. I didn't like Circe, but I felt a little sorry for her. I'd hate to face the wrath of the council. She'd messed with one of the founding families. They'd find her, eventually. And Balthazar, too. Poor Bam.

Natalie might be able to help figure out a way to restore him and Lily.

Lil kicked in suddenly with "Goodbye My Lover" by James Blunt.

I took a deep breath. "I know what happened to Lily, too," I said. I motioned to the jukebox. "That's what she's been trying to tell me. Lil is Lily."

"You've got to be kidding," Mr. Bone said. "She was under our noses the entire time? Impossible."

Lil played "Man Smart, Woman Smarter" by Robert Palmer.

"I think she's trying to tell you something," Samantha said wryly.

"I'll be darned," Mr. Bone said.

"What do we do now?"

"Don't breathe a word of this to anyone," he said. "I must consult with the council."

I started to protest, but Mr. Bone cut me off. "We shouldn't be hasty. We have to make sure that we can restore Lily without doing any harm. There are some spells with some nasty counterattacks built in."

I nodded, reluctantly. "Can I at least tell my family?"

"Yes. The council relies on their help and we trust them implicitly. Now, I must be going. Good work, Daisy, Sam," he said. He took a last sip of coffee and then paid the bill and left.

Sam yawned. "I'm beat. This detective stuff is hard work."

"Me, too," I said. "I'm ready for a nap."

Once I was back home, I headed straight for bed. Information swirled around in my brain until a piece of the puzzle clicked into place, but I was already tumbling toward sleep.

CHAPTER **TWENTY-TWO**

I was still napping a couple of hours later when my cell rang and jerked me from a sound sleep. An unfamiliar number appeared, but I picked it up, anyway.

"Hello?"

"Daisy, it's Lilah Porter. I thought of something. It may be nothing."

"You never know what little detail may end up being significant," I said, encouraging her.

"It's about the boarding school that my parents are sending me to."

"Go on," I said.

"My dad let it slip last night that it wasn't exactly his idea," she said. "In fact, Ms. Tray is the one who encouraged them to send me there."

I gasped. "That's horrible."

"I know," she said. "Ms. Tray really seems to dislike me. In fact" — Lilah hesitated, then seemed to make up her mind about something —"she dislikes a lot of the kids at Nightshade who are different."

"By different, you mean paranormal?"

"Exactly."

"Thanks a lot, Lilah," I said. "You've been a big help. Are you still leaving?"

"Tomorrow," she said miserably.

I didn't know what I could say to cheer her up. "Hold off on leaving as long as you can," I said.

"What difference does it make? Either way, I'll have to go."

"Maybe not," I said. "If my hunch is right, people will be embarrassed that they ever listened to Ms. Tray."

After I hung up with Lilah, I sat on my bed and tried to figure out what my next move should be. I was pretty sure I knew who the blackmailer was. But now I needed to prove it.

I needed to get back into the school, but it was the weekend, so it was probably locked up tight. I wanted to take a look at a certain guidance counselor's office.

What Lilah had just told me made me certain Ms. Tray was the blackmailer.

I called Samantha. "I need to get into an office at the school," I said. "But it might be dangerous."

"I'm in," she said. "I'll be there in ten minutes." She hung up before I could thank her.

The school was deserted, but that didn't stop us. I hesitated. "I don't want you to get into any trouble," I said.

"Don't worry about it," she said. "We won't get into any trouble. At least, not if you manage to find out who has been sending all those letters," she added.

I stared at the door, willing the lock to click open. It did and Sam and I entered the school.

As soon as I stepped in the room, I knew I'd found our blackmailer. The hearts. There were hearts all over her office. That's why the seal's design had looked so familiar.

The minuscule triple-heart design was repeated in the cushions in Ms. Tray's office, on the painting hanging on the wall, and on her personal stationery, which didn't match the creamy white stationery the blackmailer had used. Unless she'd written the blackmail notes at home, I was sure I'd find the wax-seal stamp in her office somewhere.

I went to the file cabinets first. "Try her desk while I look here," I told Sam.

I went through the files, but I didn't find anything that would link her to the blackmail.

"Did you find anything?" I asked Sam.

"Not yet," she said. "Hey, this drawer is locked."

I crossed to the desk and knelt next to her. "Did you see a key anywhere?"

"Nope," she said. "Why don't you, you know?" She crossed

her arms and made a little blinky face, like the woman in the bottle in that old TV show.

"I'm not a genie," I said. "But maybe I can use my psychic powers to open it."

I concentrated on turning the lock, and a minute later, it clicked open.

Samantha yanked open the drawer. We'd found what we needed. In the drawer was creamy white stationery, red wax, and an embosser with three tiny hearts.

"C'mon, let's go," I said. I grabbed the stuff and shoved it into my bag.

"You're not going anywhere," Ms. Tray said. She was standing in the door of her office, but when we looked up, she shut the door and locked it.

"We were j-j-just . . ." Sam stuttered.

"Please do not insult my intelligence," Ms. Tray said. "I know what you two naughty minxes were up to."

I crossed my arms and faced her. "You can't stop us. We know you were the blackmailer."

"Who would believe two girls over a well-respected counselor?"

"Chief Mendez, Mr. Bone, pretty much everyone in Nightshade," I said.

She frowned. "I'm afraid you're right about that. Your kind does stick together."

Your kind? That sounds like the Scourge rhetoric.

"This does pose a problem. What will I do with you?" Her smile made my stomach clench. Despite her sweet tone, there was a threat in her words.

"It was so convenient," I said. "As a guidance counselor, you found out everyone's secrets and used your position to blackmail."

"That was a little sideline. A very profitable one," she said.

I glanced around the room and my eyes fell upon the La Contessa purse. I pointed to it. "You blackmailed Circe into giving you that, didn't you?" I said.

She smirked. "It looks better on me than it ever did on her."

Sam said, "You don't have the personality to carry a purse like that off."

"A lot you know," Ms. Tray said.

"We know more than you think we do. We know you were working for the Scourge."

"My main job is more like a recruiter, actually," she said smugly. "But manipulating parents into sending their spawn away was useful. Divide and conquer works every time."

"A recruiter?" Samantha said.

"Yes, for an organization I'm sure you're very familiar with," she said. "I was trying to recruit your boyfriend."

It dawned on me what she was talking about. "You were trying to recruit Ryan into the Scourge? But you sent him a blackmail letter."

She shrugged. "Merely a fishing expedition," she admitted. "I had nothing on him, but sometimes a little nudge will get one of my little friends to spill the beans."

"Friends? You don't know the meaning of the word," Sam hissed.

"I have plenty of friends," she said. "And they'll take care of Nightshade. You'll see."

I was trying to keep her talking while I sent a telepathic message to Rose. *Help.*

She chuckled. "I'll miss blackmailing y'all. Those notes were so much fun to write."

"Words have power," I said. "The power to hurt."

Bea Tray's face grew animated. "You understand, then."

"You *want* to hurt other people? Your students? People who trusted you?" I couldn't believe it. "Why did you convince Penny to write those things on the bathroom wall?"

"That girl was so malleable," Ms. Tray said. "Brain like putty, honestly."

"How did you find out which students were paranormal?" I asked. Samantha and I edged closer to the door.

Ms. Tray grabbed me by the shirt front and slammed me against the wall. My head spun for a second.

I tried to focus on something so I wouldn't throw up. "This," I slurred, "is my favorite shirt."

Sam started forward, but I shook my head.

"Trying to keep me talking?" Her smile was as syrupy as

ever, but it was giving me the major heebie-jeebies. "They warned me you were tricky," she said.

"Who did?"

"My clients. The people who are going to pay me very well for the information I've gathered about the citizens of Nightshade."

"But you promised the people you blackmailed that if they paid you, you'd keep their secrets," Samantha said.

Her smile grew even wider. "That's the thing about blackmailers, my dear. They just can't be trusted."

I figured something out. "You're going to sell the secrets to the Scourge, aren't you?" I said. I probably shouldn't have opened my big mouth, because Ms. Tray's eyes flashed for a second and her southern belle façade cracked open. What I saw there in her eyes made me shudder.

"Daisy, what am I going to do with you?" she said, advancing toward me. "I just can't let you leave here and give away all my secrets, now, can I?"

I was wishing for a giant set of bleachers at about that time, but no such luck. The room was empty, except for Ms. Tray's overdone decorations, which didn't seem like they would be of much use.

I sent out another SOS to Rose, but knew that even if she heard it, she might not be in time to save Sam and me.

Beatrice smirked when she saw me glancing around the

room. "I heard what happened to your cheerleading coach," she said. "You don't have any weapons, but I do."

She held up a long slender knife. It looked like it could filet me in about a second. She warned me. "Don't try anything tricky with those powers of yours or your friend gets it first."

"Gets what?" Sam said. Then she saw the knife and shuddered. "What are you going to do with that?"

Beatrice smiled. "Bless your heart," she said. "I'm going to kill y'all with it." She grabbed my hair and dragged me over to the window.

"What are you doing?" Sam said.

It hurt, but I gritted my teeth. "You can drop the phony accent," I said. "We know you're not from Atlanta." I waved my hand in front of her.

"You've been a busy little bee, haven't you?" she said, without a trace of a drawl. Her real voice sent splinters of fear down my spine. This was not a helpless southern belle.

She moved closer to the window, taking me and pieces of my hair with her. She'd clearly been anticipating that I would try to use my psychic powers. But in desperation, I gave her a head butt WWF style. For the first time, I was thankful that Ryan liked to watch pro wrestling on TV. My head rang with the force of the blow, but it slowed her down long enough for me to use my powers to bring the knife to my hand.

"Samantha, go get some help," I said. The hand that held the knife was shaking, so I used my other hand to steady it.

"But I don't want to leave you," she said.

"Just go. I'll be fine."

I kept one eye on Ms. Tray as Sam took off at a run.

Ms. Tray hissed, "You won't do anything with that knife. You don't have the nerve. It's all there in your files. You're weak."

She came toward me and I dropped the knife. She bent down for it and I grabbed a plaster cupid. I brought it down on her head and she crumpled to the floor. I kicked the knife away from her.

"File that in your Rolodex," I said to her prone form. "I may not use this knife, but I'm not weak."

She was so still that, for a moment, I thought I'd killed her. Would Principal Amador expel me? I thought wildly. After all, this wasn't the first staff member I'd attacked, even though I'd had plenty of good reasons.

Sam ran back into the room, followed by my sisters and Ryan.

"Are you okay?" he said.

"I'm fine," I replied. "But I'm getting tired of people underestimating me."

Samantha said, "They really need a better screening process for the staff at Nightshade."

"Seriously," I replied.

Ryan hugged me so hard I couldn't breathe. "Hey, I'm okay," I said. "Or I will be if you let up a bit."

He looked hurt, so I whispered so only he could hear. "Werewolf strength, remember?"

"Sorry," he said. He hugged me again. "You scared the life out of me."

Samantha said, "I called Chief Mendez and he's on his way."

"Dad is going to flip out," Poppy warned.

"Do we have to tell him?" I asked.

"Of course we have to tell him," Rose said. My sister looked stern.

"I was just kidding," I said. Mostly.

"What should we do with her in the meantime?" I asked.

Ms. Tray groaned and sat up. She lunged at me, but Ryan stepped in front of me.

"Don't try that again," he snarled. His eyes turned yellow and Ms. Tray's face went slack in shock. Recognition dawned in her face.

"You're one of them," she said with loathing.

"Not such a great recruiter for the Scourge, are you?" Ryan said. "Couldn't recognize a werewolf when he was standing right in front of you."

"Ryan, do you think you should say anything?"

She lunged again and I jumped back. Outnumbered or not, she still scared me. Ryan grabbed her arms and restrained her, but she kicked him in the shin.

"We should tie her up," I said, but, fortunately, Chief Mendez arrived while we were looking for rope.

He read Ms. Tray her rights and cuffed her. Officer Denton escorted her down to a waiting squad car.

We followed them outside. My heart was still racing, but my hands had finally stopped shaking.

"Daisy, thank you for getting to the bottom of this," Chief Mendez said. He hesitated and then said, "I called your parents to let them know I was en route."

I groaned.

"I had to tell them," he said. "Your father worries about you, and I don't think I could look your mother in the face if anything ever happened to you. Or my son."

Ryan gave my hand a squeeze.

"I've done all right so far," I said defensively.

"You've done an excellent job," the chief said. "But please, for me, be a little careful."

"I will," I said. "If you'll do something for me."

"What is it?" he asked cautiously.

"Talk to Lilah Porter's parents," I replied. "They're shipping her off to boarding school."

He seemed a little reluctant until I added, "At Ms. Tray's recommendation. Lilah didn't do anything wrong, except take a midnight swim."

"I'll send Officer Denton to do it," he said. "He knows Lilah's mother."

"She's a, a swimmer, too," I said, trying to delicately convey that I knew Mrs. Porter was a mermaid.

He gave a wry grin, which reminded me so much of Ryan's smile.

"Officer Denton will talk to them," he said. "But I can't guarantee they'll listen."

"I hope they will," I said. "The best place for Lilah is in Nightshade. With her friends."

Chief Mendez said something to Officer Denton and then the officer took off in a separate squad car.

"Boy, almost getting killed makes me thirsty," Samantha said. "Want to go to Slim's to get some coffee?"

"Sure," I said. "But first I have to make a quick phone call."

I punched in the number and waited for it to pick up. "Lilah, it's Daisy. Hold on. The cavalry is on the way."

"What was that all about?" Ryan asked.

I linked arms with him. "I'll tell you all about it at Slim's."

I was holding hands with Ryan when Dad and Mr. Bone arrived. On reflex, Ryan dropped my hand, but I linked our hands again. He gave me a sheepish grin.

"Daisy," Dad said. "We heard what happened. Are you okay?"

"I'm fine, Dad," I replied. "It's all under control."

"So what's going to happen to Ms. Tray?" Poppy asked.

Ryan's dad said, "She's been arrested and is cooperating with the authorities. That's all I can tell you right now."

"I heard she'd been gathering intel for the Scourge for years," Poppy said. "Daisy was the first person to suspect her."

The chief nodded. "That's true," he said. "She'd probably still be blackmailing people if it weren't for Daisy."

My father said, "I guess you can take care of yourself, Daisy. You suspected Ms. Tray all along, but I believed everything she said."

"I didn't suspect her at first," I admitted. "I didn't *like* Ms. Tray, but I hadn't a clue that she was involved with the Scourge."

"You're not just saying that to make me feel better?" Dad asked.

I shook my head. "Not at all. I didn't trust her, but I didn't suspect her for a long time. Almost too long."

My dad suppressed a yawn.

"It's late," I said. "Let's get you home."

"I was thinking we could grab a milk shake at Slim's," Dad said. "Or are you too tired?"

"All of us?" I said, glancing at Ryan when I said it. I still wasn't too sure if my dad's newfound trust of Ryan was going to last.

"*All* of us," Dad replied. "My treat."

Even the chief came with us to Slim's. Dad ordered enormous milk shakes of every flavor.

Since the place was almost empty, Slim came out from the kitchen, carrying a huge platter of appetizers.

"Anybody hungry?" he said. "On the house."

"I'm starving," I said.

"Daisy, are you okay? You look like you've been in a fight," Slim said.

My dad chuckled. "She has. You should have seen her before she got cleaned up."

As I sipped my shake, I wondered what the next few months would hold.

"I can't wait until graduation," Ryan said suddenly.

"Why is that?" I said. Why was my boyfriend looking forward to our possible separation?

He took my hand. "Because then we'll both go off to college and leave all this craziness behind," he said.

Poppy snorted. "Fat chance of that," she said. "This is Daisy you're talking about. She's a trouble magnet."

"Hey, I'm sitting right here," I said. "Besides, I predict smooth sailing from here on out."

"Did you have a premonition?" Rose asked.

"No," I said. "But I know I'll do my best to stay out of trouble until I graduate."

My dad put his hand on my hair. "I have confidence that Daisy can take care of herself, no matter what trouble she ends up getting into."

"Thanks, Dad," I said.

Now that the Scourge was back, there was no doubt that my senior year was not going to be the calm year I'd hoped for.

Lil was back in her usual corner. I fished out a few quarters and went to see if I could get a clue about what the rest of the year held in store for me.

I hadn't forgotten about my promise to her, either. I punched in a random selection — E17 — and waited to see what would happen. Nothing.

Lil had gone silent. No matter what I tried, she wouldn't play.

"She's pining," Flo said. "If I didn't know better, I'd say she was in love. She either doesn't play anything or she plays love songs. The depressing kind."

As if she heard, Lil broke into "Love Is a Losing Game" by Amy Winehouse. When that song ended, "Alone" by Heart came on, followed by "Since I Don't Have You" by the Skyliners.

"Wow, she is depressed," I said. Then, in an effort to cheer Lil up, I searched the song list and punched in my choice.

James Taylor's "You've Got a Friend" came on. I hoped Lil understood what I was trying to say.

It seemed she did. "Thank You for Being a Friend" by Andrew Gold came on.

I went back to the table.

"Something wrong?" Dad asked.

"Lil," I said. When he looked perplexed, I clarified. "The jukebox."

"I'm following you so far," he said.

"I know it sounds weird, but she's a friend of mine," I said. I told him about the hints Lil had given me in the form of songs.

"She's definitely special," Dad said.

"She's sad," I said baldly. "And I want to help her. I need to research ways to bring her back."

"Research?" Dad brightened. "I can help you with that."

"Awesome," I said.

"I've been thinking about writing a book," Dad said, with a shy smile. "About my experiences."

"That's great, Dad!"

The Giordano family was finally complete. My dad had accepted that I wasn't a little girl any longer and was ready to help me solve mysteries, even if it meant a little danger.

With the help of my family and friends, I'd solve the mystery of Lil's beginnings and maybe even find a way to get her out of the jukebox.

"Only in Nightshade," Ryan said in my ear.

"Only in Nightshade, what?" I asked.

He gave me a kiss, and then shrugged. "I guess we'll find out," he said.

I couldn't wait.

Acknowledgments

Thanks to all the fans who've written and sent e-mails. Your enthusiasm is greatly appreciated.

Marlene Perez is the author of *Love in the Corner Pocket*, *The Comeback*, and the Dead Is series, including *Dead Is the New Black*, which was named an ALA Quick Pick for Reluctant Young Adult Readers. She lives in Orange County, California, where rumor has it, she spends a lot of time online, or playing Bejeweled, or writing novels.

www.marleneperez.com

How well do you know the **DEAD IS** series?
Take this quiz to find out!

1. What are Nightshade High's school colors?

a. black and red

b. red and white

c. purple and pink

2. What is the first song the jukebox plays in *Dead Is the New Black*, and who is it in reference to?

a. "Big Mouth Strikes Again" by the Smiths—Penny

b. "Heartbreaker" by Pat Benatar—Samantha

c. "Here Comes Your Man" by the Pixies—Ryan

3. Where did Daisy and Ryan's first kiss take place?

a. under the stairs at school

b. at the morgue

c. on Daisy's front porch

4. What is Nightshade's school mascot?

a. sea monster

b. slug

c. squid

5. Which of the following is *not* one of Samantha's accessories when she sports her goth look?

a. wheelie backpack coffin

b. ankh pendant

c. pink skull bikini

6. What activity did young Daisy enjoy but had to give up?

a. cooking

b. gymnastics

c. fortunetelling

7. The hooded figure at the Nightshade City Council whom Daisy calls Skull is actually

a. Chief Mendez

b. Slim

c. Mort Bone

8. Which character wears a cowboy hat?

a. Cassandra Morris

b. Officer Denton

c. Beatrice Tray

9. What song is played by both Lil the jukebox and the band Side Effects May Vary?

a. "Walking with a Ghost" by Tegan and Sara

b. "Leader of the Pack" by the Shangri-Las

c. "Rock 'n' Roll High School" by the Ramones

10. Daisy first discovered her psychic powers while

a. playing Frisbee

b. making dinner

c. making out with Ryan

11. Ryan's eyes are

a. green and intense

b. blue and glassy

c. amber and eerie

12. In moments of stress or anger, Daisy's psychic powers sometimes get out of control. Which of the following is not something Daisy caused to happen?

a. a bag of popcorn kernels exploding

b. the contents of a candy dish shooting into the air

c. the phone flying out of Poppy's hand

13. What is the name of the boutique where Sam works?

a. Tete de Mort

b. Ye Olde Coffin Shoppe

c. Shifters R Us

14. Gage's ghost haunts

a. the Eternal Rest Room

b. the Tranquility Room

c. Poppy's bedroom

15. The Giordano girls break into which teacher's house?

a. Mr. Krayson's

b. Miss Foster's

c. Mr. Davis's

16. Two of Daisy's favorite treats are

a. milk and cookies

b. chocolate and coffee

c. celery and peanut butter

17. What gift does Ryan give Daisy for her seventeenth birthday?

a. a gold locket that once belonged to his mother

b. an ankh bracelet

c. a kitten

18. Samantha's dad looks like which movie star?

a. Tom Hanks

b. Robert Pattinson

c. George Clooney

19. Who was Penny's junior prom date?

a. Duke Sherrard

b. Wolfgang Paxton

c. Tyler Diaz

20. Where did Daisy vacation with her mother, grandmother, and sisters the summer after her junior year?

a. Romania

b. Italy

c. The Jersey Shore

21. When she returns from vacation, Daisy is surprised to find her boyfriend has more

a. facial hair

b. muscles

c. money

22. Which slogan cannot be found on any of Flo's T-shirts:

a. "I LIKE CHILDREN—FRIED."—W.C. FIELDS.

b. WOMEN WHO PAY THEIR OWN RENT DON'T HAVE TO BE NICE

c. NO PARKING ON THE DANCE FLOOR

23. A doppelganger of which Nightshade resident is in a cage at the city council meeting?

a. Miss McBennett from the post office

b. Mrs. Wilder, elderly matriarch of the Wilder clan

c. Mrs. Mason from Daisy's mom's garden club

24. Daisy gives cooking lessons to

a. Poppy

b. Nicholas Bone

c. Natalie Mason

25. Which movie did Rose watch over and over when she and Nicholas broke up?

a. *Truly, Madly, Deeply*

b. *An American Werewolf in London*

c. *House of Dracula*

26. From whom does Daisy first hear the gossip that her father is back in town?

a. Penny

b. Samantha

c. Slim

27. Rose's summer job with Dr. Franken requires her to visit many

a. farms

b. bakeries

c. nuclear power plants

28. Ryan and Sean get into a fight during a game of

a. football

b. baseball

c. Scrabble

Answers:

1. b; 2. c; 3. b; 4. a; 5. c; 7. c; 8. a; 9. c; 10. b; 11. a; 12. c; 13. a; 14. b; 15. c; 16. b; 17. a; 18. c; 19. a; 20. b; 21. b; 22. c; 23. a; 24. c; 25. b; 26. a; 27. b; 28. c

Lil says:

24–28 correct: "Superstar" by Lupe Fiasco
You know Nightshade so well, you might as well be on the Nightshade City Council!

18–23 correct: "Wonderful" by Adam Ant
You could be a resident of Nightshade. See you at Slim's!

12–17 correct: "Somewhere Around Midnight" by Airborne Toxic Event
You're ready for a little midnight mayhem. Keep reading!

11 or fewer correct: "Borderline" by Madonna
Just like Daisy, you need a little practice!